The Turn

Jim Surmanek

To Patsy, who urged me to learn the fantastic game of golf four years before I wrote this book, and to the many folks, especially the men's Geezer Golf Group, with whom I played golf for the last four years.

*Life is a heterogeneous
conglomeration of multifarious
phenomena and irreconcilable
inconsistencies.*

Golf? Similar.

Quotations to Inspire Your Life and Your Game

- "A true friend never gets in your way unless you happen to be going down."

  Arnold H Glasgow

- "Golf is a set of bodily contortions designed to produce a graceful result."

  Tommy Armour

- "In the sweetness of friendship, let there be laughter, for in the dew of little things, the heart finds its morning and is refreshed."

  Kahil Gibran

- "Try to think where you want to put the ball, not where you don't want it to go."

  Billy Casper.

- "At times our own light goes out and is rekindled by a spark from another person. Each of us has cause to think with deep gratitude of those who have lighted the flame within us."

  Albert Schweitzer

- "Golf is a compromise between what your ego wants you to do, what experience tells you to do, and what your nerves let you do."

  Bruce Crampton

- "A good friend is a connection to life --- a tie to the past, a road to the future, the key to sanity in a totally insane world."

  Lois Wyse

- "The most important shot in golf is the next one."

  Ben Hogan

- "Don't walk in front of me…I may not follow. Don't walk behind me…I may not lead. Walk beside me…just be my friend."

  Albert Camus

- "Golf is the closest game to the game we call life. You get bad breaks from good shots; you get good breaks from bad shots – but you have to play the ball where it lies."

  Bobby Jones

- "Many people will walk in and out of your life, but only true friends will leave footprints in your heart."

  Eleanor Roosevelt

- "Achievement is largely the product of steadily raising one's levels of aspiration and expectation."

  Jack Nicklaus

- "Every friendship goes through ups and downs. Dysfunctional patterns set in; external situations cause internal friction; you grow apart and then bounce back together."

  Mariella Frostrup

- "Sometimes I think I have an almost perverse love of being down, even being defeated because I know it will spur me on to greater things."

  Greg Norman

- "Friendship is the source of the greatest pleasures, and without friends even the most agreeable pursuits become tedious."

  Thomas Aquinas

- "Success in golf depends less on strength of body than upon strength of mind and character."

  Arnold Palmer

- "There is one friend in the life of each of us who seems not a separate person, however dear and beloved, but an expansion, an interpretation, of one's self, the very meaning of one's soul."

  Edit Wharton

- "If you try hard enough, anything can happen."

  Charlie Sifford

- "Friendship is a strong and habitual inclination in two persons to promote the good and happiness of one another."

  Eustace Budgell

- "On the first tee, I kept telling myself, "Trust yourself, you can do it."

  Annika Sörenstam

- "Each friend represents a world in us, a world possibly not born until they arrive, and it is only by this meeting that a new world is born."

Anais Nin

- "If you are going to talk negative about a place, you're almost throwing yourself out, to begin with, because golf is a mental game."

Jordan Spieth

- "The greatest thing about tomorrow is, I will be better than I am today. And that's how I look at my life. I will be a better golfer, I will be a better person."

Tiger Woods

- "Friendship is the hardest thing in the world to explain. It's not something you learn in school. But if you haven't learned the meaning of friendship, you really haven't learned anything."

Muhammad Ali

Chapter 1:

The Plan Kicks-off

Dave pressed the button on his steering wheel to turn off the radio. He welcomed the quiet, hearing only the whisper of the *whoosh* of the AC's cold air blowing on him as he drove 40 mph in a 45-mph zone. He slid his hands around the steering wheel as if he was polishing it and thought, *I can do this*. He needed to squelch thoughts of failure lest it put him on a different path.

A loud popping and crackling noise pulled him out of his thoughts and warned him that a car was about to pass him on the left lane of the two-lane street. Dave glanced to his left and saw a young driver smirking, exhibiting his expertise at downshifting. The driver honked his horn, raised his middle finger, and sped past him.

Idiot, thought Dave. *If you want to kill yourself, keep me out of it!*

Fifteen seconds later, the middle-finger honker driver and Dave were stopped at the red light. Dave snorted, wanting to tell the driver he wasted gas and didn't save time. *What was the point of all that juvenile stupidity?* He shook his head and called out to the driver, knowing he couldn't be heard: "The red light is telling you something, jerk." That gave him some satisfaction of sorts, though.

Not a second later, he remembered something. "Bella!" he shouted and quickly dialed her number. After a few rings, Bella picked up the call. "Hi, this is Dave Martin. I forgot to tell you not to come today. Can you make it in a few days? If you can't, next week is fine."

"I'm not scheduled to clean your house until Friday. In two days," said Bella.

She would have seen the blush on his cheeks if he and Bella

had been face-to-face. He was miffed that he carefully planned every detail for the day but forgot to call her, and he was doubly miffed that he forgot which day was cleaning day. "Y-Yes, of course! I was confused about the days. See you on Friday. Bye." He disconnected the call quickly, saving himself from further embarrassment.

The dashboard's digital clock showed 3:05; His wristwatch didn't agree. *3:10? I'll go with 3:10. Better be early than being late. Reset the clock later. Or is my watch wrong?*

A yellow sign with red crisscrossed flags stuck at the top of it read, "Lane Ends Merge Left." As the two lanes were about to merge into one, he glanced at his speedometer and was satisfied that 30 mph was a safe speed since the nearest car in the left lane was four car lengths back. He clicked on his turn signal and started to merge when he noticed the car behind him pull out to pass him. He turned off his signal and let the car pass, but the car didn't, allowing Dave to move left. Dave thought, *Yeah, you just saw the sign and changed your mind. Good guy. Smart.*

When the one lane opened to two, he noticed a sign at the intersection: No U-turn.

He played a word game and spoke to it: "No, You Turn." *I can't,* he thought. *He needs me, and I'll be there for him.*

Two joggers on the sidewalk also stopped at the stop light but kept jogging in place. *Is that called jog idling?* he thought and smiled. They appeared young, maybe mid-twenties, and in excellent physical shape. *I looked like that. Yeah, fifty years ago.* He leaned to the right and looked into his rearview mirror. As he stroked back his wavy, almost white hair, he thought about dying it so he looked younger but then shook the thought for some reason. "Nah, you look great," he gently said to his reflection and immediately forcefully clutched his steering wheel and bellowed, "Stop it, jerk! Focus!"

The light turned green. Dave accelerated. The joggers turned around and started to jog in the direction they came. "No, you turn. I can't," he said with a severe tone.

Thoughts raced in his mind. *I wish I didn't have to do this. I wish things were different. I wish Nicole were here.* He was on auto-pilot, subliminally aware of the road signs, traffic lights, and other cars, but when his mind clicked off from *thinking* to consciously paying attention to his driving, he wondered how his mind could do that.

"Made it," he muttered as he drove in circles on the spiral ramp at the Sky Harbor parking lot. One level up, the LED sign read: 27 Spaces Available; Level 2 showed 47.

Nope. Level 4 will have the most spaces, and I'll get one near the elevator. As calculated and expected, he found a spot five spaces away from the entrance to the elevator bank. He walked through the dimly lit lot to the elevators that would take him to the arrival gates. Still in good shape for a 70-year-old, he could have jogged but thought fast-walking was safer, especially after he got plantar fasciitis a year ago playing pickleball.

Stepping around a McDonald's take-out bag with some fries, he wondered why people couldn't throw garbage into garbage pails. He shook his head and made unintelligible sounds. *Why the hell do I care?* He looked at his watch again.

Dave didn't pay any attention to the guy beside him on the elevator. The doors closed. The elevator dropped an inch, stopped, jolting the two passengers, and descended smoothly. The ceiling light flickered. "Damn. Is it broken? Are we stuck?" Dave frowned, looking at the flickering lights, unaware that he had said those words out loud.

"What?" said the other passenger.

"Huh?" Dave turned to the passenger. "I didn't say anything."

"Yeah, you did. You talking to someone on your phone?

Bluetooth?" the passenger asked, pointing at his ear for emphasis.

Dave realized he must have been talking aloud to himself. His cheeks were slightly flushed. "Yeah, Bluetooth," he answered to hide his discomfort.

As a people person, he never wanted to disrespect anyone, and arriving late was a sign of disrespect. Being on time for this meeting was of paramount importance. He was about to meet his lifelong friend. If he were late, it could have sent the wrong signal. It could have caused anger, anxiety, or any number of negative emotions. He knew he was about to have a tug-of-war with Brian and had no way of knowing he would also face another tug-of-war.

Every fiber in his being told him he needed to intervene and help. He tried many times in the last few months, but his efforts were fruitless. He thought a face-to-face was the best way to solve the problem. He needed to lie about his reason for inviting Brian to Phoenix. He rationalized that there would be no meeting if he told the truth. He didn't know that Brian also lied.

At the arrivals level, the flight board showed Delta-Seattle-Phoenix-Arrived. He approached a guy wearing a Delta uniform and asked, "If it just landed, will the passengers come out this way?"

With a deadpan tone, the Delta employee said, "Yes, unless they jump off the plane and run across the tarmac."

The joke didn't sit well with Dave, but he didn't comment and offered a quick and courteous smile. Guessing that Brian packed lightly for his two-day visit and had a carry-on bag, Dave quickly walked around the terminal looking for him, hoping he would find him sitting on a bench or looking at store windows. Nowhere to be found, he returned to the elevator banks to go down to baggage claims. *Up, down. Good metaphor,* he thought.

The directory in baggage claim showed Brian's flight unloaded bags at carousel #5. Dave dashed as quickly as he could, saying sorry several times as he elbowed around the crowd of passengers, many of whom wrestled with their luggage as they tried to leave the terminal. At carousel #5, he eyed passengers on his left, right, and on the other side of the carousel. He didn't see Brian, so he did what he could at the time: wait.

As the passengers grabbed their bags and the crowd thinned, Dave saw Brian standing still, in a daze as bags circled before him. He looked like the Unabomber photos Dave saw during the 1990s. Brian needed to be with Dave, his best friend, his lifelong friend with whom he shared good times and bad times, happiness and sorrow. Brian was always there when Dave needed help, and Dave was always there for Brian. But this time was different. He felt like a two-ton boulder was pressing down on him.

Brian watched the bags moving past him and counted how many were of each color: one *black, two black, one red, one blue.* A gentle squeeze on his shoulder and a "Yo!" jolted him back to reality. He turned around, seemingly surprised that it was Dave. Dave frowned at his surprise, wondering if he was expecting someone else. He didn't know what to make of Brian – *Is he in a fog? Dementia?* But whatever daze he was in, Brian snapped out of it, and a guy-like hug and back-smacking followed. Dave felt the hug was more cordial than genuine.

Dave said, "You old fart. Glad you made it."

"Yeah, me too, I guess." Dave was taken aback by the "I guess" but chose not to pursue it.

"I got here a few minutes ago but didn't see you," said Dave.

"I was here. Right here. Didn't move," said Brian with an incredulous stare. "You know too much sun can ruin your eyes."

Dave took a step backward. He fanned his arm up and down Brian. "You're not Brian, are you?"

Brian pulled back his hoody, removed his sunglasses, and,

without a hint of humor, said, "What are you talking about?"

"For starters, Bri, the hoody. Just about every time I saw you, you'd be dressed in a shirt, pants, and shiny shoes. You even kept your golf shoes shiny. I think you owned more Tommy Bahama silk shirts than Nordstrom had on its racks. You were the epitome of a natty dresser."

"Natty? You're dating yourself with that word," said Brian as he gave Dave a quizzical look.

Dave raised his eyebrows and said, "Okay. Stylish, cool, kumbaya, whatever. Never mind."

"So, can't a guy wear something different for a change?" Brian shrugged, hoping Dave would drop the topic.

Dave gave him a fist bump on his shoulder. "Of course. It's just that I didn't recognize you in a sweatshirt, a hoody, sweatpants, and flip-flops."

Brian said, "Good for traveling. Nothing gets wrinkled."

Brian looked gaunt, thinner than Dave remembered when last he saw him. His well-trimmed, nearly white beard took a turn for the worse and looked scraggly. "I see you gave up shaving."

Brian stated that razor blades were expensive. Dave correctly believed that Brian's answer was more *I couldn't care less about my looks* than an honest reason for letting his beard grow. He knew Brian was extraordinarily well-heeled and could afford to buy a razor blade factory.

The last time he saw Brian was six months ago. At 6'2" and weighing about 170 lbs., he looked healthy and in great shape for his age. "On a diet, Bri?" asked Dave.

Brian didn't want to answer any questions, let alone questions about his life. He stopped discussing his appearance without telling Dave to shut up. "Maybe I lost a few pounds since I saw you last. That's all." Brian, again, tried to shrug off the question with a brief answer.

"A few pounds times ten if you ask me," Dave said, emphasizing his point by looking at Brian up and down once more.

Sternly, Brian responded, "I didn't ask you."

Taking a half-step back and raising his palms toward Brian, he said, "Well, okay."

The way Brian sounded on the phone during the many calls Dave made to him in the last three months could not have been mistaken. Brian used to be a light-hearted, gregarious jokester but was now a sullen, relatively quiet, and almost humorless man. Of late, Brian's typical one-line witticisms were replaced by one-line nondescript comments or, as was just the case, one-line put-downs.

"Flight, okay?" Dave asked, trying to keep the conversation going with short and general questions.

"Quicker than driving."

"Yeah, but you always used to drive."

"Charlotte made me drive."

"Never knew that. I thought you enjoyed the leisure of a drive, taking in the landscape."

Brian stopped talking and stood still, looking out into space. It was the kind of look people have when viewing memories in their mind's eye.

"Bri?" said Dave, but Brian didn't answer. He just kept looking out, apparently at nothing, acting as if he was catatonic.

Dave spoke louder: "Bri!"

"Yeah, the landscape. Asphalt, road signs, trees, all that stuff. The flight was okay. I think we got in early."

Concerned about Brian's unusual behavior, Dave spoke gently. "I know. That's why I didn't meet you at the gate. Traffic and road repairs. Took me longer than it should have. And you arriving___"

"They do that, ya know."

"What's that? Who does what?"

"Airlines," he said with an accusatory tone. "They say a flight is supposed to land at, let's say, one o'clock. But they know it will probably land fifteen minutes before that. So they land early, and the pilot says, 'Welcome to wherever the hell we are, and good news folks, we did such a great job we landed ahead of schedule.' You've heard them say that, haven't you?"

Dave never heard Brian talk the way he was talking. He was an upbeat guy, rarely criticizing anyone or anything. He was the kind of person who doesn't talk about anyone unless he has something nice to say about them. Brian sounded not only very negative but also off-kilter. He had a look about him that if a mugger stabbed him, he would say *Hmm. Looks like I just got stabbed.*

"Not in those words, but yeah, I heard pilots say that," said Dave.

"You're here. I'm here. Let's go," Brian said, gesturing to Dave with a slight nod.

"Luggage?" Dave asked in confusion.

Brian spread his arms, spun around slowly, and said seriously. "I'm wearing all I need."

Dave was fifty-fifty about Brian's seriousness and had to ask. "Are you serious?"

Brian let out a *Ha!* and said, "Hell no. Loosen up."

Loosen up? He's acting like a jerk. How the hell can I loosen up?

"What color, Bri?"

"Tangerine with a splatter of puce, or black. I can't remember."

Dave wanted to accept his answer as being humorous but wondered if it was another put-down. He snorted and said, "Those are my two favorite colors.”

Brian grabbed a black suitcase and quickly returned it to the carousel when he realized it wasn't his.

“There's another one coming, Bri. It looks like that one.”

“No, not mine.”

Dave noticed Brian's foot tapping as he nervously fingered his beard. “It'll get here. Just takes time for the guys to unload the plane,” said Dave.

“I should have used the pink one.”

Dave knew Brian was referring to Charlotte's suitcase. It was decorated with her artistic touches and was easy to spot wherever it was. He refrained from expressing his thought: *Pink doesn't move faster than black.*

Dave pointed to another black suitcase and asked, “Is that yours?”

“Which one?”

“The black one.”

“They're all black, amigo.”

A young fellow passenger reached around Brian and grabbed the suitcase that Dave had pointed at. “Yo,” said Brian. “Are you sure that's yours?”

“Yeah, old man.” He turned the tag on the handle to reveal his name. “Is that your name or mine?”

Brian stretched out his arms with his palms pointing upward and said, “I am so happy for you that you have a name, you pretentious twerp!”

The man dropped his suitcase, got into a fighting stance, fists clenched, and said, “I don't know what you said, but I didn't like it.”

Fearing a fistfight, Dave quickly stepped between the two men and said to the man, “Sorry, bud. My friend is just having a terrible day. Okay?” He slightly twirled his finger against the side of his head to reinforce that Brian was in no position to fight.

"Yeah, okay." As the man left with his luggage, he gave Brian a middle finger, which Brian fortunately did not see.

Dave grabbed the next black suitcase he saw, checked the name tag, and said, "Aha."

As Brian took his suitcase off the carousel, Dave would have expected him to say, "You have good eyesight," but got "Where to now?"

Pointing with his head, he said, "That way. Here, let me wheel that sucker for you."

"Okay, okay. Have it your way. Just because I had a few drinks and a couple of muscle relaxants on the flight doesn't mean I can't wheel a suitcase. But what the hell? You're my host, so you're in charge of my laundry. Where are we going?"

Dave was annoyed by Brian's behavior yet tried to convince himself that booze and pills might have been the cause. His best friend had just arrived after a three-hour flight to visit him when he probably didn't want to do anything but stay at home, watch mindless stuff on TV, and drink scotch. He gave Brian a pass on his behavior.

They walked through the crowds of passengers and greeters, avoiding wheeled and carried suitcases as best they could. "Are you my grandpa?" said a young girl who looked up at Brian as they approached each other.

Brian uttered a harsh "No!" Her head bowed, and her eyes shot up to look at him as her chin trembled slightly.

Dave knelt and spoke to her eye-to-eye. He asked where her mother and father were. She turned around to see where they were when she heard someone crying out, "Annie! Annie!" and hurried away toward the voice.

"A bit heavy, Bri?" Dave asked as Brian fidgeted with the tie strings on his hoody and looked away at the signage around the baggage claim area. He uttered *Hmm* as if he was surprised by the information shown.

"Okay, bud? What are you looking at?" asked Dave.

"She surprised me. It's really noisy in here. Let's go."

"Sure."

They walked gingerly to the elevators, not speaking another word until they stood in front of one of the elevator doors. Brian asked, "Are we up or down?"

Dave understood the question but chose to hear it with a different meaning. He was like a ten-year-old who had just scored a goal for his soccer team and a ten-year-old goalie who had failed to block the kick. "Up."

Exiting the elevator, Dave clicked his remote. The stop lights on his car flashed. "Right there, Bri."

"New car, Dave?"

"Uh-huh. I got it last month. I figured I owed it to myself to have a reliable car. The old one kept on needing this or that fixed." Realizing that his car could be a helpful analogy applicable to Brian's emotions, he continued, "There comes a time when you just have to face reality and make some changes." Brian was mute, threw his suitcase in the back seat, and got into the car.

Brian kept looking out the side window, turning his head occasionally as they passed people, stores, or signs, and whispered, "Of course. Stupid. Give it up. No surprises."

Dave couldn't decipher what Brian was uttering and asked, "Talking to me? See something?"

Brian jerked his body to his right and screamed, "Stop!"

Confused and concerned, Dave hit the brakes and yelled, "What?" as he focused on the road in front of him, thinking he was about to hit something. A millisecond later, he looked out the window Brian was looking out and saw nothing but a tree-lined street, then immediately jerked his head toward the rearview mirror, hoping the car behind him stayed well behind him.

"Sorry. I thought I saw…I don't know. I thought I saw something. Forget it. Let's go," Brian said, shaking his head, not sure what to say that would explain his sudden outburst.

Dave looked at him in concern but decided not to push it. From his experience in the last few minutes, he knew Brian was not really up for a chat, let alone a heart-to-heart, and spilling out what was bothering him. So, he pursed his lips and, without a word, continued to drive.

Chapter 2:

Memories Bringing Up

Dave pulled into the pebble-coated circular driveway of his house in Paradise Valley, unloaded the suitcase, and walked toward the front door. Brian followed suit and came out of the car but stood behind the opened car door and held the top of it as he stared at the house. His eyes were riveted on the front door, but he didn't see the door; it was a woman. His thoughts took him to the time when he saw her, or so he believed when they were driving from the airport. But soon, he realized it was only a woman who resembled Charlotte. This time, a vision popped out of his memory banks, an image of Charlotte waving hello and standing at the doorway.

Seeing that Brian had not followed him, Dave looked behind and saw him staring at the door. Concerned, he trotted back to the car and looked at the door, trying to figure out what Brian was looking at. "You okay, Bri? Drinks catching up?"

Dave's voice pulled him out of his memories, and he shook his head a little. He paused before stammering, "I'm fine. Just tired. Let's go inside." Brian wasn't fine.

Dave frowned. He but didn't want to confront Brian with what he said, but his concern outweighed his decision. "Sure, let's get inside. Are you sure you're okay?"

Brian's face contorted into an annoyed expression. He didn't like Dave probing. His voice was slightly raised when he said, "Dave, I'm fine!"

Dave could clearly see Brian was frustrated, so he decided to drop the subject, but now he was sure that there was indeed something bothering Brian.

As they approached the front door, Dave wanted to lighten up Brian's mood and said, "So, what do you think of the paint job?

"You got me there. What paint job?"

Dave waved his arm across the facade. The last time you were here, the house was stark white. Nicole didn't like the stark white, so I had it painted with a color called *warm neutral.*"

"You mean beige?" Brian said, raising his brow.

Dave shrugged and said, "Well, yeah, I guess you can call it beige. But it's called *warm neutral.*"

"They charge more for that?" Brian inquired, genuinely curious about the cost of the paint.

"More for what?" Dave asked in confusion.

"The paint."

Non-confrontationally, Dave asked, "What are you talking about? Yeah, painters charge for the paint."

"If the painters used beige paint instead of *warm neutral,* would the paint job have been cheaper?" Brian repeated to get his point across.

Dave smiled. He wanted to open the door to a conversation, not slam it shut. "Ya know, I think you're right. Would have been cheaper."

Dave entered the house, gesturing Brian to follow, and he straight away went to the guest bedroom, believing Brian would want some rest after traveling. He tossed his suitcase on the bed and looked around. "I like the very light blue walls in this room," he said. Laughing out loud, Brian continued, "Or is it called *sky blue on a misty morning?*

Even though he pegged Brian's raucous laughter as forced, Dave was delighted he was loosening up. "You're not going to let it go, are you?"

"Yeah, okay. Enough. I'm going to unpack. See ya downstairs in a minute," Brian said, raising his hands in surrender to tease Dave a little.

Dave shook his head and smiled, saluted Brian, and left the room. He was happy that the *old* Brian was still inside what appeared to be a changed Brian.

Brian first unpacked the framed photograph of Charlotte and placed it on the nightstand. After putting his travel pouch in the bathroom, he looked around—*A night or two. No biggie,* he thought.

He wanted to stay in his room and reminisce but decided to be a gracious house guest and join his host downstairs. Dave was sitting at the built-in mahogany bar and raised a can and the bottle. "Dr. Pepper or scotch?"

Brian replied, "Glenfarclas," and took a seat beside Dave.

"I don't speak Gaelic," Dave said matter-of-factly.

"It's scotch."

"Ditto," Dave said, putting Dr. Pepper back into the fridge. "I grew up in Brooklyn. English, well, some kind of English was spoken, and some Yiddish, Spanish, and Italian. But not Scottish.

With an Irish accent, Brian said, "No, laddie. It's nary a language. It be a brand of scotch."

Dave chuckled, delighted with the leak in Brian's emotional armor. He wanted to play along with the Irish accent but didn't have the linguistic talent to do so. "Glenfarclas sounds more like a curse word than a brand name."

Still keeping his Irish accent, Brian told Dave, "Go Glenfarclas yaself and fetch this old bugger any swill you might be havin'."

The fridge spewed ice into two glasses, and Dave poured a healthy amount of Dewar's scotch into both. He handed Brian his drink. "Here ya go. And, by the way, it's good to see that you haven't lost your sense of humor."

Brian didn't respond; he only pursed his lips and clinked his glass against Dave's. He nodded and said, "All the best, my friend."

Brian took a long, slow swallow and let out a very audible *Ahh*. "This is a good one," gesturing at the drink.

They left the bar with their glasses and sat on companion dark brown, well-worn, soft leather lounge chairs. Brian held his drink and twirled his wedding ring around his finger. He looked up at the ceiling but not to see if he could see any cracks in it.

The sight was not lost on Dave. He thought he could delve into Brian's thinking and asked, "Does my ceiling need a painting?" He continued with the paint topic, as Brian was pretty cool about it earlier. Dave thought it would be a good icebreaker.

Brian said, "Hmph. Maybe. How's your lovely wife?

Dave hoped Brian would have responded to his question by saying something about his thoughts about Charlotte and how he was feeling at that moment. But his attempt to get Brian to open up seemed to have failed. He responded, "Nicole's fine, absolutely fine. She's spending a week in Flagstaff with Missy and our grandkids. She hasn't seen them for a few months, and not seeing them drove her crazy."

"Facetime? Skype?" Brian asked, moving his gaze from the ceiling to Brian.

"Yup, she does that, but as she has said, you can't give a very good hug in two dimensions."

"Did she choose this week because I was coming here?" He glanced sideward at Dave and said, "Because Charlotte wasn't coming?" Brian wasn't smiling and certainly not laughing when he asked the questions. There was a burr of harshness in his tone as if he felt like Nicole didn't like him.

"No, not at all," said Dave calmly. "It was the kids' idea to visit them now. She just went along with what they proposed."

Brian nodded, seeming to have accepted Dave's explanation as he sipped his drink.

"I love what Nicole said when she knew she wouldn't be here

when you arrived," Dave chuckled as he continued the conversation.

"What?" Brian asked, curious to know what she had said.

"She said to tell you that you can fart anytime you want, and you don't have to apologize," Dave told him, clearly amused.

Brian gave a small, forced smile and said, "Hmm. Very considerate lady you got there."

"Dinner? Want me to barbecue a steak, or do you want to go out?" Dave asked, putting his empty glass on the side table.

"Steak sounds good," Brian nodded as he finished his drink and added, "Medium rare, if you remember."

"I do," Dave said and got up to fetch the steaks, leaving Brian with his thoughts. Dave turned the gas on the BBQ and pressed the ignite button. He thought *If only it were this easy to light a fire under Brian.*

Brian remained in the family room and poured himself another glass. Sipping, he called out to Dave, "When do you want to talk about money? And my trust? And what's the news you wanted to tell me face-to-face?"

"All in good time, Bri. Now's the time for relaxation and a ribeye. And I'm sure you came across some great jokes you haven't told me yet," Dave answered as he cut some French beans to go with the steaks.

Brian sat up from the lounger while Dave tossed the steaks on the grill.

"Sorry, Dave. I know I'm acting like an ass. And it isn't the alcohol that's doing it," Brian said in a low voice, ashamed for being harsh to Dave earlier.

"No prob, Bri. I know you've been through a lot. God, I don't know what I would be if Nicole…I mean…hell, you know what I mean," Dave said, turning to him and shaking his head. He couldn't find the right words to express his sadness.

Brian stood up and walked toward Dave. He put his drink on the counter, wrapped his arms around his best friend, patted him on his back, and said, "You *are* my best friend, you asshole."

"Thanks, Bri. Right back at you, except without the *asshole*," Dave said, patting him back.

***

The evening wore on while they chatted about inconsequential happenings as they devoured the delicious steaks Dave had prepared for dinner. Dave understood Brian's erratic temperament when he laughed at one memory and nearly cried when he recalled a different one. His emotional ups and downs challenged Dave to understand without telling him to stop and get over it.

"Do you realize we've known each other for six decades?" Brian asked.

"Well, to be exact, Bri, it's been fifty-seven years," Dave said as he pointed his index finger at Brian.

"Okay. Fifty-seven years. You accountants are so…I don't know. Precise?" Brian said, not sure if that's the right word.

"I'm not an accountant, Bri. I'm an estate planner and financial advisor."

"And I'm glad you're not. I wouldn't like you then," Brian replied jokingly, and Dave was almost pleased that Brian was acting almost normally.

Dave's face lit. "Yeah, we were thirteen when we met. *Thirteen*, Bri!"

"Long time ago, wasn't it? About fifty-seven years ago, if my math is right."

"I'll ask my accountant to check your math."

"Yuk, yuk," said Brian. He held his drink in front of himself, twirling the ice cubes around his glass, looking at it as if a movie about

Charlotte was playing.

Dave broke his train of thought. "Remember how we met?"

Brian's pupils danced as he recalled the event. "Yeah, I do. Times were different then. Life was different. Ha! All I thought about back then was having as much fun as possible. Didn't care about the consequences. You know, *To hell with the torpedoes, full speed ahead,"* speaking in a gruff, commanding voice, thinking that's how Admiral Farragut would have sounded.

"Damn the torpedoes. Full speed ahead," Dave hollered.

"That's what I said," Brian said with a raised brow.

"I was just stating the exact quote," Dave shrugged.

Brian scrunched his face and said, "Why?"

Dave's eyes opened wide and said, "It's in my nature to be precise, I guess."

"You *are* an accountant!"

It seemed Dave was walking on eggshells while talking to Brian. He sensed that the conversation was going in the wrong direction and changed the subject. "Yeah, junior high school. Basketball. Farmer," Dave said, hoping that Brian would remember him.

"Farmer?" Brian asked, trying to remember who he was talking about.

"He was our gym teacher. He introduced us."

Brian closed his eyes and shook his head. Dave couldn't make head or tail of what Brian's gesture meant, but before he probed, Brian abruptly said, "I decided to call it a night. I'm off to bed. Night."

"I'm going to bed too," Dave nodded, sensing that Brian had had too much to drink and it would do them no good if he pushed further. "Oh, you can raid the stuff in the bathroom cabinet in case you forgot to bring anything. Like deodorant or ear wax remover. Whatever. Hasta morning," Dave added.

In his room, Brian undressed down to his skivvies. He sat on the bed, called Charlotte, and heard her message. *If you dialed correctly, you reached me. Please leave a message.*

"Hi. It's late. I'm in bed. Everything's okay, but I guess you knew that. Call you tomorrow. Love you. Night," Brian whispered and ended the call.

After completing his five-minute dental hygiene routine, washing up, and putting on his pajamas, he sat at the side of his bed. Looking at Charlotte's photograph, he whispered, "Good night, my love." His fingers touched his lips and then the photo.

He stared vacantly at the ceiling. The room was dark, except for the moonlight that sneaked in between the window shutters, but his thoughts were brightly lit. It felt more like a reliving than a simple glance at the past. He smiled when he relived the first time he met Charlotte, and kept smiling when he saw himself getting married. Shivers went up his spine when he envisioned her at the altar. He remembered the laughter they often shared and could still hear those waves of laughter in his memories. He thought that no man could have been happier than he was.

***

Dave lay in bed in the master suite down the hall, thinking about the last several hours with Brian. He texted Nicole: "If UR up, call me."

A minute later, Nicole called. "Hi, babe. How's it going with Bri?"

He gave her a fifteen-second synopsis of the evening, ending with, "I could be kind and say he's troubled, conflicted, in an emotional upheaval, but the only word that fits right now is whacko."

"I suggest you be kind, love," Nicole understood what he meant but reminded him to be patient with Brian.

"I think I'm batting a hundred, maybe two hundred. Some of it's working. Some of it seems to be falling on deaf ears," Dave sighed in frustration.

Nicole said, "It's not surprising how a broken heart orders your ears to become deaf."

"I know, I know. It's just disheartening to see him this way. Maybe if I kick him in the ass, he'll get the message," Dave let out a dry chuckle.

"Brilliant, Dave. Make sure he bends over before you kick," Nicole said sarcastically.

"Great idea. Maybe when he's teeing up his ball," Dave joined in the joke.

"Just stick to the plan and get him involved in all of those memories…those *meaningful* memories," Nicole reminded him.

"Yeh, I started doing that. I brought up how we met fifty-seven years ago in high school. That basketball thing." He heard Nicole yawn. "Tired or bored, love?" he asked.

"Tired. Long drive. The grandkids knocked the crap out of me with all of their games. Running games, hiding games, and catch-me games. *Ugh!* Tomorrow, I will try to teach them how to play chess."

"Good luck with that."

"High school?" she asked.

"I figured starting with the oldest memory and slowly bringing up more of them as the years went by would be a good thing," Dave said thoughtfully, hoping that would work.

"Could work. Or maybe let the circumstance dictate your memories bringing up?" Nicole suggested.

"You *are* tired. Memories bringing up?" Dave chuckled incredulously.

"Ha-ha, yeah. I'm going to bed now, love. It'll work out. You're doing the right thing, and when you do right, things turn out right. Nighty night." With those words of encouragement, she ended the call.

He put the phone on the bedside table and lay in bed, thinking about what buttons he should push tomorrow. He wondered if Brian had an ignite button.

With a long sigh and flickering hope, Dave smacked his pillow, rested his head on it and tried to turn off his brain.

Chapter 3:

The Gane We Call Life

Brian stared in the mirror and reflected on his wet, naked body.

Frowning, he thought, *Why the hell did they put in such a large mirror? I look bad enough when I can only see my face.* He sucked in his stomach, keeping his eyes on the mirror, and turned sideways.

Nodding his head and raising a brow, he thought, *Not bad for a hundred-year-old man.* But his eyebrows drew together, and his eyes saw nothing as his mind raced, wondering why he even cared about how he looked. *I don't give a shit.*

With that, he let his stomach loose to its original form and walked closer to the mirror, stopping a few inches short of it. This time, he stared into his eyes, finding nothing but hollowness. As he kept staring, his thoughts transformed, becoming more serious and…. dangerous.

What's it all about, Alfie? Why doesn't it just end? It's going to end soon, so why not now?

But soon, the gloomy voice was interrupted by a loud "Yo! Breakfast!" It was Dave. Brian sighed, not knowing whether he should be thankful for the interruption or irritated.

Shaking his head, he faced the mirror again. He ran his fingers through his beard. *Scraggly? Yup, scraggly. So what? Well, for Dave. Let's do it.*

He walked to the bedroom door and opened it to call down to Dave, "Need ten minutes! Fifteen." and then shut it back again.

Hygenized, as Brian would call it, he dressed and followed his nose to the origin of the sizzling bacon scent.

When he reached the kitchen, he was glad to see what his nose told him. "Bacon! I knew it. Haven't lost my sense of smell."

Dave chuckled at his enthusiasm and said, "And good morning to you. Coffee's over there."

He looked to where Dave had pointed and saw what looked like a fancy machine that makes coffee. "Is it voice-controlled?" he asked.

Dave laughed. "No, I didn't get the one with voice commands. Here, let me brew a cup for you." Dave stopped flipping bacon strips and lowered the flame so they didn't burn as they sizzled in the pan. He then walked to the coffee machine and helped Brain brew some coffee.

Brian looked around the kitchen as the coffee maker gurgled. Everything was organized and neatly displayed. He noticed a pen on the counter and frowned slightly; it was the only thing he saw that looked out of place.

"You forgot the pad," he said to Dave.

"Pad?" Dave asked in confusion. The coffee maker binged when Brian's cup was filled.

"Never mind," said Brian. He shook his head and asked, "Where's the machine that puts sugar in the cup and stirs it?"

Dave knew he was being sarcastic, so he just gave him some sugar packets and a spoon with a friendly smile, letting Brian know that he knew what he was playing at. Just then, he noticed something. "Hey, you shaved. I haven't seen you without a beard for___"

"Big deal, I shaved. I wanted to look…I don't know…" Brian shrugged, not knowing what to say as he himself wasn't sure why he decided to shave. Instead, he changed the subject, "You have any eggs?"

He held up two eggs and said, "Up, over easy, or scrambled?"

Brian didn't answer. Dave cocked his head, his eyebrows lifted, and he said, "Up, over easy, or__"

"I heard you," Brian said, a bit annoyed, but then added with a smile, "Just trying to remember what I had yesterday. Don't want to have the same thing two days in a row."

Dave accepted his clown smile and smiled back. "I think you should have them raw. Goes better in a weird way with a clean-shaven face."

Brian pointed his finger at Dave and said, "Rocky."

"I don't get it. What's rocky?" Dave asked, tossing an egg in the air and then catching it.

"What Rocky Balboa did in 'Rocky,' the movie. Crack them open into a glass and drink 'em."

Dave's brows raised slightly in realization, and he laughed, saying, "You'll have to run up the steps at the capital."

Brian uncharacteristically didn't reply. Dave squinted while trying to remember which steps Rocky had run up. He then thought how stupid it was to want to know which steps. "Being a good friend, I'll give you a pass on the steps. So, how do you want your eggs?"

"Whichever. Doesn't matter, but make it three," Brian said as he stirred his coffee and took a sip.

Dave melted butter in a frying pan and let it warm a bit. He then cracked open an egg and let it splat on the pan. He looked at the sizzling egg, bright yellow yolk surrounded by glistening egg white; he recalled how Charlotte loved to make and serve bacon and eggs. Two sunny-side-up eggs were two eyes. A long bacon strip, the mouth. Some parsley for eyebrows.

He smiled at the thought and decided to surprise Brian, but not a second later, he decided against it. If he had served his breakfast that way, it would have screamed 'Charlotte.' *Now is not the time for reminders,* he thought.

"You got it. I'm making scrambled eggs, bacon on the side," Dave informed, and Brian simply nodded. Noticing that Brian was silent, he told him, "Hey, take a look outside. Great sunrise, isn't it?"

Brian looked outside and decided to enjoy the early morning air. Grabbing his coffee, he meandered through the exquisitely designed large kitchen toward the back patio. It was six o'clock. The rising sun lit the few clouds with streaks of pink and gold. The fronds on the palm trees surrounding the backyard were at the mercy of the gentle breeze. They were in silhouette against the sun, and if not for the swaying fronds, one might have thought Brian was looking at a gigantic mural – clearly painted by God.

He raised his eyes to the heavens and thought, *Nice job with the scenery, but I hate what you did to me.*

No sooner than Brian finished his cup of coffee, Dave went to the patio with a tray stacked with food. He stood by the table while still holding the tray and gazed out. He had the same feeling that Brian had – a beautiful view and then some. "Nice, no?"

"Yeah, I guess. It looks just like Seattle, except our sky is more grayish, the air colder, and we don't have many palm trees." Again, a deadpan statement from Brian.

Dave snorted and said, "Yeah, Bri. Seattle and Phoenix could be twin cities, like Minneapolis and St. Paul. For example, what we have in common is one hundred twenty degrees in July, right?"

"It reaches one-twenty in Seattle only if you stand near a burning building. And we have a lot of those lately," Brian added.

Dave needed to get back to the seriousness of the situation, so he said, "I was thinking about how we met all those years ago."

"Fifty-seven years ago, Dave. *Not* six decades," Brian rolled his eyes as he took a seat and placed his almost empty coffee cup on the table.

Dave didn't know if Brian was trying to be funny or giving him crap for his comment yesterday. He decided to smile. "Yeah, those were days."

They reclined in their chairs, holding their refilled coffee cups with both hands, and reminisced about how they met.

***

Mr. Farmer, the high school science teacher who doubled as the boys' gym instructor, blew his whistle to get the attention of the twenty students on their first day in the gym. He said, or more like hollered, "We're going to limber up with some basketball passing!"

He had the students lined up in two rows of ten each, with the rows facing each other, ten feet apart. He instructed the first student to pass the ball to the kid opposite him and told the kid who caught the ball to toss it to the next kid in line opposite him. "It's easy at first. There's only one ball. It gets harder. Trust me."

The tossing back and forth happened until the last boy in the row caught it.

"Now, two balls." He gave a ball to the first kid. As soon as he tossed it, he gave him another ball. All went well. "Now, three balls." The more balls, the more laughter. It was an instructional exercise, but the kids thought it was a fun game.

Dave tossed his ball to the kid opposite him, but in doing so, he couldn't give the needed attention to the ball that Brian tossed at him. It hit Dave in the head and knocked him off balance. Brian laughed. Dave grimaced, picked up a ball, and was about to hurl it at Brian aggressively when Mr. Farmer blew his whistle, and the tossing stopped.

He pointed to Brian and Dave and told them to go and sit by the stack of cushioned floor mats piled in the corner. The rest of the students continued with the ball passing. "Keep it going. It's called *passing*. It's not dodgeball," Farmer said, making sure that Brian and Dave listened to him.

At the mats, Farmer lectured Dave and Brian on the benefits of exercise, the need to focus on what they're doing, and the fact that accidents happen. "They're called *accidents* for a reason," he said. He ended his chat by telling them about sportsmanlike conduct. "Now give me two laps, and you can get back to the warm-up."

As they jogged around the gym', Brian asked, "You okay?"

Dave's head didn't hurt one bit. Only his ego. The other kids laughed when they saw Dave wobble after getting hit in the head. Laughter is a good thing, except when it is directed *at* you.

"Yeah. Fine. Why did you think that was so funny?" Dave asked, clearly not ready to let the incident go.

Laughing, Brian replied, "You did look friggin' funny, like a drunk guy."

Dave quickly thought of Brian's statement and started wobbling like a drunk as he trotted. He said, "You mean like this? `

Brian nodded and laughed again, clutching his stomach. Dave joined him. Farmer heard the laughter and was glad they were getting along, obviously putting the incident behind them.

Dave and Brian walked back to join the other students. "I'm Dave."

"I'm Brian."

"What are you doing after school?" Dave asked.

"Don't know," Brian shrugged.

"See ya later, then?" Dave said, holding out his fist for Brian to bump.

"Sure." Brian did a fist bump, threw his hands up with open fingers, and uttered the sound of an explosion.

***

Dave finished his breakfast as he remembered the first time they had met. Brian hardly touched his.

"What changed, Bri?" Dave asked in a small voice. Not getting any response, he continued. "Why was it so easy to solve a problem when we were kids and so hard now?"

Still waiting for a response, Dave tried a third question, "Do you have any idea what happened to Farmer?"

That got some response from Brian, and he blinked in confusion, "Who?"

"Farmer," Dave repeated.

"Farmer?" Brian was still confused, not remembering who Dave was referring to.

"Mr. Farmer, our gym teacher," Dave added, hoping that would help Brian remember the teacher.

Brian raised his brow, suddenly remembering the teacher, and said, "He's gotta be in his nineties. Maybe he's a centenarian. Probably has Alzheimer's."

Dave realized he was heading down the wrong path by using the story of their basketball accident as a device to help Brian face reality. So he tried to brush off the topic and said, "Yeah, maybe so. Just a thought. Let's clean up. And by the way, nice word, centenarian."

"Yeah. I always wanted to use that word sometime. Cognomen is another one," Brian said with a chuckle.

'I'm not going to ask," said Dave.

"It's more or less a nickname," Brian said anyway.

Dave scrunched his face and said, "Who the heck would call anyone cognomen?"

"Ha!" said Brian. "It's not a nickname. It means nickname."

"Glad you told me. Made my day," Dave said a bit sarcastically.

"And you? What word did you always want to use?" Brian asked out of curiosity.

Dave shook his head, "This is right up there with the ten most ridiculous conversations I ever had."

"Fine." Brian sat still in his chair, staring at his empty coffee cup. Except for his eyes still open, he looked like he was sleeping.

Dave spoke up. "I got a word. Mercurial."

Holding his coffee and plate of unfinished breakfast, Brian stared at two hummingbirds pecking away at the feeder, sucking up the sugar water. He thought, *Life's pretty simple for you guys, isn't it?*

Brian ruminated about *mercurial*, concluding that it was unfair to Dave to be all over the place with his words and actions. "Good word, Dave. I've taken it to heart."

Hoping that Brian might be softening, Dave thought it might be time to continue his campaign to help Brian break out of his shell and move on with life. "I don't want to wax philosophical, Bri, but I find what Bobby Jones said about golf being a metaphor for life is true."

"What?"

"Golf is the closest game to the game we call life," said Dave.

"Heavy," Brian said. His comment seemed genuine, but Dave thought it might be a pleasant way of saying he didn't want to talk about it anymore. He poured himself a third cup of coffee, looked at his watch, and said, "Okay, okay. Wax away."

Dave pushed on. He needed to open many doors…to get inside Brian's head and help him escape prison. "Simple. You have good shots and bad shots, good moments in life and bad moments. You encounter obstacles and get around them. You hit your ball___ "

"Yeah, I get it. It's like the weather. The sun rises, and it's a new day. Yesterday is gone. We can think about what happened yesterday but can't undo it. If yesterday had shitty weather, it doesn't mean that today will also be shitty. The weather changes. Life changes," Brian concluded, letting Dave know he got his point.

Dave wanted to scream *Yes!* but decided to say, "Exactly, Bri. Life goes on."

"Hmm," said Brian as he rubbed his index finger around the rim of the coffee cup. "Good shots, bad shots. Made me think…"

Dave leaned forward, anticipating a revelation, but Brian pivoted and said, "You know why it's called golf?" Dave had heard that question and the answer many times but thought it best to play along. With a smile and a *huh,* he said, "Because the F-word was taken?"

Dave's elated reaction to Brian's take on golf and life turned on a dime. He clenched his fists and curled his toes to contain his emotions. He didn't know if he should laugh at the cliché or try to steer the conversation back to being serious. He had all he could do not to grab Brian by the throat and shake some sense into him. He finally calmed himself, knowing that forcing Brian to man up and take a hard and realistic look at his situation was counter-productive. He hoped that Brian fully understood what he was trying to tell him about his life – his yesterdays and tomorrows. *He needs time to chew on it. I know Brian can turn things around. I pray he does.*

Looking at the clock on the kitchen wall, Dave said, "We gotta leave if we're going to make our tee time. Let's get going. But think about what I said."

"I'm thinking, Dave. Let's go," Brian said, putting the empty coffee cup on the kitchen counter before following Dave outside. Three steps later, he returned to the coffee cup and placed it in the sink. "There you go," he said. "Everything in the right place." *No, not yet,* he thought.

Chapter 4:

Last Game

The weather could not have been better for a game of golf: an almost cloudless sky, eighty degrees, low humidity, and only a trace of a breeze. It was the kind of day that reinforced Dave's decision to be a snowbird, living in Chicago most of the year but avoiding the cold and snow by residing in Paradise Valley on the outskirts of Phoenix most of the winter. He and Nicole bought their home five years ago as part of their retirement plan. Whenever any of his friends up north told him he was crazy for moving to the desert, he would always quip, "I don't have to shovel the sun."

"Welcome to Palms, sir," said the attendant as he unloaded the golf clubs from Dave's trunk.

"Palms?" asked Brian, clearly confused by the name.

"Uh-huh. It's a new course; well, a refurbished course. Remember the one we played at five years ago, right after we bought our house here?" Dave reminded him.

"Sure do," Brian nodded, his brows raising in realization. "The one with rocks, trees, sand, dirt, mud, and a patch of grass here and there," he added as he looked around in hopes of seeing the familiar grounds.

"That's the one. It sure was a dog track. It was bought out and fixed up. I thought we'd give it a try. You know, to try something new." Dave hoped that playing on a new course would help reinforce his objective of convincing Brian that things change in life – new challenges, new accomplishments.

"I wish we could have played at your club," said Brian. "I kind of got used to it in the last few years."

"I hear ya," said Dave. He was a bit disappointed that his ploy didn't seem to sit well with Brian at first, but he was confident it would play well as they circuited the eighteen holes. "Tell you what. Let's play a few holes here. If you don't like it, I could get a tee time at Legacy." Dave laid out the options for Brian, hoping that he would at least give the new place a shot and that his plan wouldn't go down the drain immediately. Before Brian could reply, he paused and conspicuously rubbed his stomach, looking uncomfortable. A resounding, unmistakable sound escaped, capturing Dave's attention. He had farted.

Dave stopped abruptly to turn around, looking at Brian with a raised brow. Chuckling, he waved his hand vigorously in front of his face and said, "Good one, Bri," as his face scrunched a little, just to tease Brian. "I think the geese on the lake heard you calling them."

"Yuk, yuk. Too much coffee, I guess." Brian shoved the blame on the coffee Dave had brewed him that morning.

Dave just shook his head sarcastically, "Sure."

Brian ignored him and signaled the attendant. "Where's the men's room?" The attendant pointed, and Brian walked away."

***

While washing his hands in the men's room, his eyes fell on the mirror in front of the washbasin, and he stared at his reflection. After three seconds of staring, he flicked water droplets at his image. "You're all washed up, buddy. One more round, and that's it."

Exiting the men's room, he saw two arrows on the hallway wall. One pointed to 'Golf,' the other to 'Lounge/Restaurant.' Having about thirty minutes till tee time, he decided to check out the lounge. He remembered the old one that could have made an excellent setting for a turn-of-the-century cowboy flick with Will Rogers spewing political one-liners. The place was as run-down as the golf course.

Following the arrows and after a few steps, he entered the completely remodeled lounge and was pleasantly surprised. It was brightly lit, but the glow seemed more reminiscent of candlelight than the harshness of electric bulbs. Scattered around were comfy chairs and plush sofas, inviting relaxation. Funky, hand-crafted wood tables with turquoise stone inlays added a unique and modern touch to the overall aesthetic. Amidst these, bronze statues were reminiscent of Remington's sculptures.

"Nice, isn't it?" said a waiter that approached him.

Brian nodded as he kept looking around, savoring in the little details added to the lounge, "A lot different than what it used to be. The whole place gives me a nice feeling."

"Yeah," said the waiter. "Sometimes change can open your eyes to something better."

There was something about what the waiter said, perhaps the emphasis on embracing the change or something. Or maybe it was the tone. Brian didn't know, but it sure made him ask, "Are you a friend of Dave Sherman?"

"No. I'm new here and don't know everyone yet," the waiter answered.

"Aha," Brian nodded. He wished the waiter a good day and left to join Dave.

***

Waiting for Brian to return, Dave called Nicole to update her. "Morning. Sleep good, babe?"

"I haven't slept this good since the last time I slept this good," Nicole yawned. "You?"

"Ditto," Dave said and looked around to see if Brian was back. "We just arrived at Palms. Brian is evacuating his large breakfast of two fork-fulls of scrambled eggs and nearly a whole pot of coffee,"

Dave updated, and Nicole chuckled. "He's everywhere with his emotions. Up, down, sideways, backward, and very little forward. The guy's manic-depressive," his tone shifted to a more serious and concerned one.

"Patience. Time," she said. "Remember what Charlie Lamont told you?"

"I know. No confrontations. Ease him along," Dave repeated, assuring that he remembered all of the advice he was given.

"He also said that if you try to shake some sense into him, all you'll wind up with is a very shaken guy," Nicole added, reminding him that it would require a lot more patience than he initially thought.

Not that he didn't agree with Nicole, but he just wanted his friend to be back to his usual old self. The need for patience was agonizing for him, yet he knew that helping Brian was impossible without it. "Shrinks certainly have a way with words. Everything okay with the kids?" he asked, changing the subject.

"Couldn't be better. I'm thinking of staying here for a few months. Tell Bri you want him to live with you while I'm gone," Nicole replied.

"Great idea, honey. But I'll have to get rid of all the knives in the kitchen," Dave pursed his lips.

"Yup, good idea. Gotta go. Enjoy the game. Ciao," Nicole cut the conversation short, clearly in a hurry to go about the day.

Dave fiddled with his clubs, jiggling them in their golf bag compartments. It had no effect other than killing time waiting for Brian, which seemed to be a long time. His first thought was that Brian was dealing with a problematic biological situation. *Constipation? Diarrhea?* His second thought was more concerning.

His pace increased from a walk to a jog when he went to the men's room. He called out to Brian and swung open three toilet stall doors. There was no response, and the stalls were unoccupied. Brian wasn't to be found. *Where could he be?* he thought as he jogged further to the lounge and went inside. Brian wasn't there either. Concerned that he might have left not pleased with the renovated place, he raced back to the golf car only to see Brian already there, sitting in it. He let out a sigh of relief, panting a little from all the jogging, "Hey, Bri. You okay?"

"Fine. And dandy, sugar candy," Brian said in an almost singsong voice but an expressionless face, making Dave quirk a brow in surprise. He saw and heard two Brians; the old one that started singing and perhaps dancing to the tune of *"Fine and Dandy,"* and the other Brian, the one in front of him who delivered a dry statement.

"I wondered what happened to you," Dave said, joining him.

"I went on a tour. Have you seen the new lounge these guys put in?" Brian said, turning to him.

"Yes. No, but I'll check it out later." Dave needed a minute to compose himself and went to the bucket of water to soak a couple of club-cleaning towels. He dipped the towels into the bucket, rung them out, and dipped them again. *Smack him with a wet towel? Kick him in the ass? Can I actually help him?*

His thoughts were interrupted when he heard Brian yell out, "Yo. Wet enough?" Dave signaled him with two fingers, indicating he would take two minutes.

At the golf car, Brian was inspecting the two sets of golf clubs harnessed to the back of it. He pulled the driver out from Dave's golf bag and yelled, "TaylorMade. New clubs?"

Dave walked to the car and said, "I bought them last week. I haven't used them yet."

Brian pointed to the slightly dull marks on the driver's face and said, "You bought them used?"

"No. New," Dave shook his head.

"Then who hit some balls with them?" Brian asked as he

inspected the clubs.

"I did," Dave nodded.

With a contrived sardonic tone, Brian said, "Aha! Caught in a lie. You *have* used them."

"Very funny, Clouseau!" He put his hands together in front of his chest and feigned sorrow. "I'm innocent. I'm innocent. Hitting balls on the practice range is *not* using them."

Brian picked up on Dave's Clouseau and spoke with a French accent. "This time, mon ami, I will overlook your misuse of words. But I will be like a Komodo dragon and carefully observe you."

"Komodo dragon?" Dave asked as he started to drive the car around.

"It's more memorable than a hawk," Brian shrugged as he put the clubs back in the bag.

Dave snorted and told Brian he had a bizarre mind. It also registered that Brian was opening up. He thought, *Is his humor coming back? Is that a sign that I'm getting through to him? Is he tugging less on the rope?*

Dave pointed to the other set of clubs and said, "These are my old clubs. Ping. The last time we played, you borrowed my Callaway clubs. These Pings are better and newer."

Brian let out a big "Heh!"

"What's the translation of 'heh'?" Dave raised a brow.

"The last time we played, I beat you. I used your old set. Callaway. Well, I guess it's now your old set once removed or your old-old set. Now you want me to use the Ping clubs you used when you lost to me. Right?" Brian said.

Dave gently pinched Brian's cheek. "You clever dog. You've uncovered my plan to destroy you on the course."

"I don't care what clubs I use. I intend to beat your ass, clubs aside." Acting like a cavalry commander ordering troops into battle,

Brian pointed his golf club out to the golf course and said, "Charge!"

Dave's first thought was George Custer at Little Bighorn, but he quickly discarded the thought when 'last stand' came to mind. "What are we playing for? I mean, what are the stakes? A million a hole, as usual?"

"Yup," Brian nodded.

"If memory serves, I owe you a million," Dave tried to remind him, but Brian already had a comeback ready.

"Two. You forget that you owed me one when we played in Chicago, and then you also lost when we played in Seattle a year ago," Brian reminded him.

Dave was tempted to say he had a ledger of wins and losses back at the house, which he didn't, and chose to say: "I did forget that. Seattle was a disaster."

Brian didn't comment, and Dave noticed his demeanor began to take a quick turn without warning. His emotions were like a light switch: on, off, on, off. He sat there looking straight ahead as if he was in a trance. "Bri?" Dave called him, but Brian didn't respond. Dave hit the brakes. "Bri? What's up?"

After a few seconds of silence, Brian responded. "When you mentioned the last time we played in Seattle that it was a disaster, it was. And so was the next day. It was the day Charlotte got home from the oncologist and told me..." He couldn't finish his sentence. Gulping, he wiped his teary eyes. "Sorry."

Dave put his hand on Brian's shoulder. He knew there was nothing he could say to ease the emotional pain Brian was experiencing. He just wanted to be there for his friend and know he had a friend.

Brian cleared his throat loudly and shook his head. "What the heck are you waiting for? Let's get going."

Dave nodded and started to drive once again to the first hole.

They arrived at the first tee box, and Brian began to put his golf glove on as if it were the nitrile glove he used in his dental practice. He tucked his fingers in tightly, opening and closing his hand several times to adjust it so the glove felt like an extra layer of skin. Grabbing a tee, a ball from his pocket, and a driver from the golf bag. he sauntered to the tee box while looking only at the configuration of the hole. It was a slightly elevated tee box looking out over a straight 450-yard fairway. To the left and right was a line of tall trees. Dotted in two places on the fairway were sand traps. To the left of the trees on the left was the car path; to the right of the trees on the right was a creek.

"They did a nice job on this hole," said Dave."

Brian didn't comment on Dave's comment but said, "Did you know we have a trade agreement between Washington and Arizona?"

Anticipating what he hoped would be a joke, Dave smiled. "No, I didn't know that. What's traded?"

Brian explained that in Seattle, they uproot a whole bunch of trees, dig some holes here and there, and put sand in them. They dig up the grass to make the holes and ship it along with the trees to Arizona. In turn, Arizona ships sand, which is put into the holes.

"Well, thanks for the trees and grass, Mr. Seattle. I hope the sand we send is agreeable with the Seattilian golfers?" Dave responded.

"Seattilian?" Brian looked at him, confused.

"Sounds sexier than Seattlean, no?" Dave shrugged.

"It's Seattle*ite*, not Seattl*ean*. Okay, Phoenician?" Brian said.

"Actually, it's Paradise Vallyan. Or Paradisian." Dave paused, waiting for a comeback, but didn't get one.

Brian took a few practice swings while still eyeing the fairway. "Ya know, I haven't played for nearly a year."

"Excuses, excuses. You have muscle memory. I'm sure you're

still a ten handicap," Dave joked.

"Ten? More like twenty if you ask me," Brian played along.

"Okay, tell you what. We'll play net score for the round. I have an eleven handicap, and I'll give you a fifteen. Okay?" Dave suggested, hoping Brian would agree.

"Eighteen it is. I added three strokes because…well, because…screw it. Fifteen is fine," Brian waved, but it was apparent that what Brian wanted to say took a detour and hit a speed bump while traveling from his brain to his tongue. Dave thought it best to accept his words. "No, you're right. You haven't played for a while, and you're not using your clubs. Eighteen, bud."

"Yeah, eighteen. So, when I shoot eighteen over par today, I could say I was a net scratch golfer at my last game of golf," Brian told him.

Dave stepped back, needing a moment to process what he just heard. He was shocked and had to comment. "Last game?" His voice got louder. "What are you talking about?"

Brian became slightly flushed and regretted what he said. He needed to backtrack and come up with a plausible reason for what he said. He knew Dave would fight him tooth and nail to try to change his mind if he knew what Brian was thinking.

"Yeh, I'm pretty settled on giving up golf. I don't enjoy it as much as I used to."

Dave accepted Brian's reason. "Hey, if you don't enjoy what you're doing, you should stop doing it. Start doing something you do enjoy."

"Ha! For now, that's beating your ass," Brian joked as he hit the air with his club for dramatic effect.

Dave laughed and said, "Time will tell. Grip it and rip it, bud."

Brian gripped his driver and held it out to show Dave. "I'm trying a new grip someone told me would add ten yards to my drive."

Dave thought *You need a new grip on your emotions, my friend.* "Hope it works for you. Rip it, bud."

Brian swung his driver back, paused, and remained still -- the kind of stillness one would have when a photographer is about to take a photo and says, *say cheese!*

Dave found Brian's posture curious. He knew his golf swing was always deliberate and on the mark, but this time, it seemed Brian was frozen, possibly muscularly, but probably mentally. Not wanting to be accused of distracting him during the critical moment of hitting his ball, he couldn't call out to energize Brian.He decided to count seconds. At *five*, he would walk up to Brian and ask if everything was okay. *One one thousand, two one thousand, three one thousand –* Brian completed his swing with as much might as he could. They saw the ball scream forward and then fade to the right. It disappeared when it blasted through a tree — leaves rained down. "You still got it, Bri. I mean your swing. Helluva drive! Not sure about the ball. Great shot if we were playing the other hole."

Brian forced a smile and looked at his driver. "Must be these clubs you lent me."

Dave decided not to dance gently with Brian's errant shot, thinking that some more ribbing would keep Brian in a positive mood. "No, seriously, Bri. That was a great drive. The new grip worked. You should teach kids how to hit a golf ball very far and make it go through a tree."

Brian bowed his head and eyeballed Dave over his sunglasses. "Go Glenfarclas yourself."

They stomped through the high grass next to the creek, looking down between the blades for Brian's ball. Murmuring *dammit,* and *where the hell are you?* Dave wandered closer to the creek, and there it was, nestled between two rocks in the rippling water. "Yo, it's here. A little wet but retrievable."

Brian joined Dave at the creek and looked down at his ball. "I'm up shit creek, and a paddle won't help," said Brian.

Dave immediately saw the connection between Brian's ball problem and his life problem. "Hey, Bri. Another metaphor." Brian listened but paid half attention to Dave, looking at his ball with disappointment. "It's a problem, an obstacle, kind of a detour. It's not a stop sign," Dave continued.

"Enough with the metaphors. I'm still dealing with the weather one," Brian said, a bit annoyed.

Dave thought pushing Brian to realize that the ball in the creek was like many of the problems Brian faced, was the wrong strategy. "I just had a memory flash," said Dave.

"You remember when I hit a ball into a creek?" Brian asked.

Dave shook his head. "No, no. It's not that. It made me remember when we were teenagers, and you took a nosedive into the creek. When you lost a couple of your front teeth." Dave broke out into a belly laugh at the memory. "I can see it like it was yesterday."

Cringingly, Brian said, "Gee, thanks for reminding me. I was toothless for a few months and talked like a blubbering idiot who couldn't control his tongue."

Dave laughed. "The accident wasn't funny, but your speech certainly was." Whistling while he spoke, he mimicked Brian's speech. "Where'sss my toothhhh?" Another belly laugh. Brian had the urge to laugh along but suppressed it.

Dave suggested that he get his ball retriever, but Brian snickered, "Let the damn carp eat my ball. I'm taking a drop." He dropped a ball from his pocket near the creek, inbounds, and moved left and right of it, looking down at it and then up toward the green. He pointed his driver left and right, again suggesting to Dave that he looked like a cavalry commander pointing his sword toward the enemy. He pondered the odds of hitting a successful shot between the trees, chipping it high over the trees, or taking the easy chip onto the unobstructed fairway.

Dave heard him talking to himself: "Thread the needle? Nah." and a bit later, "Lay-up onto the fairway? Hmm." and finally, "Skyball over the elm?"

Dave pointed to the green and said, "It's that way, Bri. Over there, where the fluttering flag is."

"Thanks. I *was* going to aim for your crotch," Brian retorted and kept his focus on the target but paused again. His accident of sixty-odd years ago spun in his mind.

***

Christmas in Chicago's suburbs in 1966 was the kind of Christmas one sees in touchy-feely family movies. Houses were lit with colorful lights, most done simplistically with strands outlining the roof structure and windows. Some homeowners went overboard with colorful displays of Santa, reindeer, and snowmen on their lawns, surrounded by trees lit with Christmas lights. At nighttime, many towns looked like Hallmark Christmas cards that showed multi-colored lights shining on snow-laden trees.

All that happens on Christmas in many towns happened where Dave and Brian lived. If you listened carefully, you could hear kids screaming joyfully as they opened their presents from Santa. As the day drew on, snowball fights abounded. Wherever there were hills, kids were sliding down them – some on sleds, some on car tire innertubes, and some on their butts.

Brian awakened Christmas morning and was greeted by his parents with the traditional "Merry Christmas! Want to open some presents?" When Brian was twelve years old, he decided to stop believing in Santa Claus. Almost all his classmates realized Santa was a fairytale and their parents had forged his signature. He wanted to be

43

a team player and went along with their decision, even though, deep down, he liked the idea of Santa.

"Here you are, Bri." Smiling and knowing his son would roll his eyes, his dad handed him an envelope and said, "Here's what Santa got for you."

Dave rolled his eyes and took the gift. Inside the envelope was a photograph of a BMX bicycle on which was written, "Check out the garage."

Brian started to dart towards the garage door when he became a *cool kid* and slowed his gait to a walk. The shiny black BMX was adorned with a large red ribbon and a note: "*Merry Christmas. Be safe. Have fun. Love, Santa Mom & Santa Dad.*"

He stroked the handlebars and seat and liked the feel and look of it. "Bitchin'" was all he said. He thought the brass plate attached to the crossbar with his name etched was a classy touch. The bike wasn't the sportscar he wanted – he knew it would be a few years till he could get a driver's license – but it was a step in the right direction.

He ran back into the kitchen and gave his mom and dad a hug and a genuine, smiling face. "I love you, Mom. I love you, Dad. Oops, make that Santa Mom and Santa Dad."

After he quaffed his toast piled high with jam and gulped his eggnog, he told his parents he would test out his bike. "Under all that nice, white snow is ice. So please be careful," said his father. Brian should have listened, but as a teenager pumped with excitement, words of warning went in one ear and out the other.

He called Dave. "Meet me at Hawthorn Park. Gotta show you somethin'."

When he met with Dave, he noticed he also had a new BMX. "Cool, man!" He didn't realize his and Dave's parents colluded on the gifts. Both of them had their brass plate names on the crossbars.

Brian's face glowed slightly from the chilly air that turned his cheeks red, but mainly from the excitement of his impending daredevil ride down the hill. They walked their bikes to the top of the hill. Side by side, with one foot on a pedal and one foot deep in the snow, Dave yelled out, "On three. One, two, three!" Pushing off, they skidded down the hill, making a deep, jagged impression in the snow.

Brian approached the creek and yelled, "I'm going for it." Dave was a fellow lover of adventure and danger but decided to jump over the creek in the Spring when there was grass and dirt instead of snow and ice. He skidded sideways near the bottom of the hill and came to a stop. Brian didn't. His father was right about the ice under the snow. Instead of his bike flying over the creek, its tires lost the fight with the ice. Bike and boy slid at great speed into the creek. Brian was hurled off the bike and landed on the opposite bank, face first.

Dave ran to him to see that Brian's face was bloodied. "Holy shit, Bri! You okay?

As he said, "Yeah, I tink so," he realized that his tongue was not hitting any of his front teeth. His two front teeth found a new home among the creek pebbles. He touched the front of his mouth with his gloved finger and said, "I'm up duh creek and a paddle woon help."

Accidents are often turning points in life. In Brian's case, his need for extensive dental work led him to Adam Erickson, DDS. Erickson liked young Brian and treated him more like a caring uncle than a patient. Throughout Brian's half-dozen visits with Erickson, he became fascinated by the dental procedures, Erickson's skill in performing them, and very much by Erickson's tutorials about dentistry.

With a big smile and having his speech back to what it used to be before his teeth were knocked out, he took another bike ride with Dave, this time on plowed streets. "I'm going to be a dentist," he told Dave.

***

Dave guessed that Brian would risk the more challenging shot because the reward could be greater. After his bike accident, Brian didn't take risks unless they were calculated risks, promising to produce a great reward. He looked at Brian, noticing he was staring out into space, motionless, yet again. "Are you still with me, Bri?"

"Yes. I was recalling that bike ride," he said, followed by a loud laugh.

He then muttered, "I wonder if my teeth are still in that creek." Brian thought Dave's smile and nod affirmed his teeth were still in Hawthorn Park's creek, not aware that it was the reflection of Dave's joy just to hear Brian talk that way.

Brian grabbed his pitching wedge from his bag. "I was right," said Dave.

With a humph, Brian said, "Right about what?"

Dave walked over to him and asked him to wait a minute before he took his shot. "I was right about two things. I thought you'd choose to go over the trees. Looks like you will. And I was right about you and the creek."

"What the hell are you talking about, Dave?" Brian asked, clearly confused.

Dave bowed his head, the kind of bow that signaled he was thinking about how to say something. He looked at Brian and said, "Uh… well, about turning points. You had one after the bike accident. You didn't go into hiding. You fixed the problem, got new teeth, and it changed your life."

"So?" Brian prodded.

"Six months ago, you had another turning point," Dave continued, hoping that Brian would connect the bits and pieces of those revelations.

Brian stood still. His pitching wedge rested on his shoulder as he pondered what Dave said. His reaction wasn't the epiphanic moment Dave had hoped for, but it was a step in the right direction. "I hear you, but I don't want to discuss it. Okay?"

"Sure. Later. Let me get out of your way," Dave patted Brian on the shoulder and stepped back.

Brian stood in front of his ball, placed the club face behind it, took a mini-step forward, spread his feet so they were in line with his shoulders, envisioned the trajectory he wanted his ball to follow, swung his club back and then forward with all the speed he could manage.

Smack!

The ball took off in a high arc over the tree. An osprey flew from its perch, frightened by the sound of a whizzing ball. Dave observed Brian's ball skimming the top of the tree, heading directly for the grassy area between the two bunkers that guarded the green. His ball landed between the bunkers and rolled to the edge of the green.

"You haven't lost it, bro. And I don't mean that as a joke this time," said Dave. "You're on the dance floor," Dave said, clapping a little to emphasize that he was indeed impressed.

Brian had a smug look on his face, which only made Dave chuckle. Brian wiped the clubface with a wet towel, put the headcover on it, and delicately placed it in the golf bag. He treated golf clubs as important instruments, just as a surgeon would treat a scapple or a dentist a probe. Dave knew Brian's penchant for being meticulous with everything he did. Some might have thought Brian suffered from obsessive-compulsive disorder, but Dave knew it was simply Brian wanting to be careful not to make a mistake. His meticulousness served him well as a dentist, as all his patients would have testified. Dave could think of only one time that Brian was not the fastidious Brian he knew, and fortunately, the mistake was fortuitous.

Dave took his fairway shot and missed getting on the green by just a few feet. His ball hit the back lip of the bunker and casually rolled down into the sand.

***

Back in the golf car, Dave steered toward the green, driving under an elm tree. Brian looked at the large trunk of the forty-foot-high elm and said, "We sent this to you. Part of the agreement."

"Sent what? What agreement?" Dave asked.

Looking smug, Brian said, "The elm. It came from Seattle."

"Oh yeah," Dave nodded, "I made a mental note to contact my state senator to see if we could trade something else. You send us rain, and we'll send you sun. How's that?"

"Deal. Now shut up. I'm making this putt for a par." Crouching, Brian carefully lined up his twelve-foot putt. Standing, he gently swung his putter backward and forward to get the right rhythm for putting it the right distance. *Thud!* His ball began its travel to the hole. Seeing it going too far left of the hole, he waved at it to turn right. As if the ball followed Brian's waving command, it curved right and stopped inches from the hole. He walked to the ball and putted it into the hole one-handed.

"That's a par," Brian muttered.

Again, Dave saw two Brians – the inexpressive one he just heard and the other one who would have been enthusiastically *woo-wooing* for salvaging what he thought was a par after winding up in the creek.

Dave audibly cleared his throat and said, "I don't want to bust your bubble, but you're forgetting your drop back there. One-stroke penalty. You got a bogey, my friend."

"Dammit. You're right," Brian said, realizing his mistake.

Dave took several practice swings in the bunker, planted his feet in the sand, and let his wedge do his bidding. His club pounced down on the sand just behind the ball, sending it in an arced trajectory onto the green. His ball landed precisely where he wanted it to, slowly rolling toward the hole. Holding his breath, Dave had a telepathic discussion with his ball, telling it to drop into the hole. It was listening but then changed its mind and stopped inches from the hole.

"It's a gimme," said Brian. "Pick it up."

"Thanks, caballero. Par for me." Dave recorded their scores in the golf car and said, "Minus one million of debt, comin' up. I like the sound of that."

Brian cleared his throat and said, "Don't count your million chickens before they hatch, my friend. We still have seventeen holes to go."

Dave nodded and paused while he reinforced his thoughts for the day. Golf was the conduit for spending a long time with Brian so he could get into his head and, with hope, steer him in the right direction. He recalled what Nicole had told him: "Let the circumstances dictate your memories bringing up." He smiled at Nicole's convoluted grammar, which somehow led him to remember a magazine article about golf as a metaphor for life. He decided to give it a try. "Did you know golf, in some ways, is a metaphor for life?"

"I thought golf was a metaphor for the weather. No, wait. Weather is a metaphor for, ahh, a bogey on the first hole?" Brian pointed out.

Dave liked the silly banter. He played along to keep it going and simultaneously tried to deliver the serious message he wanted Brian to absorb. "Now I know what DDS stands for. Doctor of Dumb Sayings."

"Pretty weak, sonny. You're reaching," Brian mocked.

Dave sucked in saliva while wiggling his tongue, trying to mimic the sound of a recording playing quickly in reverse. "What the hell was that?" asked Brian.

"I'm rewinding my words. Okay, I'm there. Here's what I wanted to say," Dave explained.

Brian laughed, not loudly nor long, but any laugh from Brian was music to Dave's ears.

"Pay attention, Bri. I want to be serious for a change," Dave said in a serious tone.

"Go for it, Mr. Serious," Brian gestured with a hand.

"This guy wrote that golf is a metaphor for life. It begins with a lot of optimism and, of course, lots of mistakes," Dave said.

Brian interrupted and said, "Like a bike in the creek?"

"Exactly," Dave pointed at him as he said, "Then you keep practicing, keep growing up, getting better and better, more in command of the game."

It was clear to Dave that Brian was taking in all he was saying, especially when Brian said, "You're talking about middle age, right?"

"Yup. Middle age. Lots of hope, anger, confusion, happiness, regrets…you name it. All that stuff that happens in life happens on a golf course."

"Hmm," said Brian. "Let me play along with this metaphor. In a few hours, we'll be at the eighteenth hole. Our game will have ended. The game of golf and the game of life. Right?"

Dave heard Brian's reference to life-ending and chose to overlook it. Better, he thought, to stick to the positive aspects of Brian's comment than harp on the negative. "We're nowhere near the end of our round, Bri. Not in this golf game, and not in our lives."

Brian looked agitated. He stretched his arm out and started tapping the top of the golf car while tapping his foot on the floorboard. He wasn't singing a song to himself. The tone of his voice reinforced that he was upset. "But it could start raining. There could be lightning. We'd be forced to stop playing. Whallah! Adios! The game's up!"

Dave hit the brake on the golf car and discussed his metaphor.

He waited a few seconds to see if Brian would cool down. He did. "Sorry, Bri. I didn't mean___"

"No sorries, Dave. I know what you're trying to do. I love you for trying. But stop," Brian said with an exasperated sigh.

"I can't," Dave said, pursing his lips.

"Stop for now. Let's play golf," Brian said, feigning a cheery tone.

Dave recorded their golf scores for the hole and mentally tallied his success and failure rate in trying to help his friend. *He started to listen to me about life. He showed some good signs. My words had an impact on him. I'm not giving up on Brian. I'm not going to let Brian give up on Brian. Torpedoes be damned!*

Chapter 5:

Sand Angels

Dave stood on the tee box and looked out at par 3, 225 yards, Hole #2. The fairway was pristine, as if a landscaping crew had carefully clipped every blade of grass down to the same height and yanked out any trace of weeds. Flower-specked shrubs lined the fairway on the left and right, guiding the eye to the green. Dave looked down the fairway with his range finder; a small smile graced his face, indicating that he was impressed. "One helluva bunker out there. You would need a ladder to get in and out of it," he said, turning to Brian, who nodded in agreement.

Brian smirked. "Just don't get in it. I'm going to carry this ball just past the bunker, land on the green, and have it roll till it hits the pin and drops in," Brian said as he pointed at the path he had supposedly planned for his shot. "It will be a thing of beauty."

"We will see," Dave chuckled, challenging Brian.

He then took practice swings while Brian teed up and was about to address his ball. "You're taking a chance I wouldn't take. I'm going for the left side, away from the bunker, and taking an uphill putt for a bird."

"Quiet. Golfer about to tee off and show you how to play this game," said Brian. He swung. His ball went straight as an arrow, right towards the pin. The high-arced ball reached its apex, and gravity pulled it back to earth. *Plop! Hello bunker!*

Dave quietly snorted and said, "I'll call the pro shop and have them bring you a ladder."

"Here's where Glenfarclas *is* the right word," Brian emphasized as he pursed his lips.

"Watch and learn," Dave said mockingly. Brian brushed his smug expression off but kept his eyes on Dave as he hit his ball exactly where he wanted. With ample backspin, it landed on the green and rolled only a couple of feet away from its landing spot. He was faced with a ten-foot, uphill putt.

The sides of the bunker were higher than Brian was tall. He had to call on his mountain climbing skills to get into it. "This isn't a bunker, Dave. It's a cavity that was left when a meteor landed. Can you pull the pin up so I can see where the hell the hole is?"

Semi-laughing, Dave said, "That's not allowed in PGA rules, bud."

Brain gave him a smirky smile, nodded, and said, "You really want to win back the millions you owe me, don't you?"

Dave continued with the jabs. "Absolutely! You got my number." Dave walked onto the green, pulled the pin, and held it high. He called Brian, "Can you see it?"

"Got it. A lovely fried egg. Why the hell do they use such soft sand?" Brian's sand wedge dug into the sand behind the ball at the downswing, catching the ball exactly right on the follow-through.

Dave saw a small sandstorm heading toward him and stepped further away. Brian's ball hit the lip of the bunker, arced up, and landed on the green.

"Wow! Fab shot. Almost as good as the one I had on the first hole." He didn't hear any response from Brian or see Brian coming out of the bunker.

He walked to the edge of the green and saw Brian sitting in the bunker, using the grip on his wedge to scribble in the sand what appeared to be numbers.

"What the hell are you doin'? You okay?" Dave asked.

Brian had a faraway look on his face as he said, "This sand made me think of when we were on the beach the summer after graduating high school." He looked at Dave, waiting for him to catch up on what he was talking about.

It took Dave less than a second to remember the incident. The story was not in his arsenal of stories he wanted to tell Brian, but it was a good one that might help steer him out of depression and into happiness. He hoped that Brian had a fond memory of the incident, not one that Brian regretted all these many years.

***

Dave and Brian looked forward to a carefree summer without books, studying, or homework following high school graduation. The weather beckoned them to go to the beach at Lake Michigan.

Brian laid his back on the sand, fanning his arms and legs as if trying to swim.

"What the hell are you doin'?" asked Dave, clearly confused by Brian's antics.

"I'm making sand angels," Brian responded with all seriousness.

Dave looked at him incredulously, "You're a nut job."

Brian sat up, crossed his arms, and spoke to Dave as a pastor might talk to a parishioner about life's lessons. "Young man, I will teach you how to attract chicks."

"Got it. By showing them you're an idiot playing in the sand, right?" Dave looked at the masterpiece Brian had created on the sand. It looked nothing like an angel.

Brian continued his speech with his pastor-like tone, extending his arm as if addressing a crowd of followers. "Ahh, an idiot am I only to the uninformed. Those people, like you, who do not know what goes on in a girl's mind."

"Oh? Really? Sand angels attract girls?" Dave said, pointing to the angel.

"Yup." Just then, a crying toddler walked toward them. She stopped abruptly, her face flushed red with all the crying, and looked at Brian. In his sitting position, he was the same height as her. She continued to cry. Not a howling cry, but more like a lost child who needed help. Tears shimmered in her eyes, reflecting the bright sun.

"Hi there," cooed Brian as he changed his position from sitting to kneeling. Not getting any response, he looked around to see if anyone looked like they were looking for a lost child. He saw people sunbathing, some playing card games on beach blankets, and some frolicking the way people frolic on the sand. None looked like they were looking for a lost child.

"Where's your mommy, your daddy?" he asked in concern. He didn't want to scare her, so he spoke to her as softly as his voice would allow. She still didn't respond.

Dave chuckled and muttered, "Ha! You're right. Sand angels do attract girls. A little younger than you might have wanted, but your magic worked."

Brian gave Dave a look that told him he would deal with him later and turned to the little girl again. "So, how about we find your mommy?"

Whimpering, the toddler nodded. Brian took the edge of his beach towel and wiped her tears. "Wanna ride on my shoulders so you're very tall and can see all around?" She nodded.

Carefully, slowly, Brian lifted her on his shoulders, and instinctively, she grabbed his hair. "Youch! Please don't pull my hair. I gotcha. I won't let you fall." She slowly eased her grip on his hair and placed her open palms on his head when she felt Brian's hands on her legs.

"Let's take a walk," he said as he walked around the beach. Dave followed. Brian and Dave took turns bellowing as they walked,

"Hello. Does anyone know this little girl?" There were many onlookers, but none responded.

After a few minutes, a young lady screamed out. "Isabel! Isabel!"

Brian walked toward her while unshouldering Isabel. The lady reached out to retrieve her and said, "Oh, thank God!" Tenderly, she asked Isabel, "Where did you go off to?" Isabel didn't respond. She walked over to her blanket, opened the ice chest, and took out a sippy cup filled with Kool-Aid. She sat on the blanket, sipping away as if her aunt hadn't almost had a heart attack looking for her. Brian chuckled at the kid's calm demeanor.

Speaking in a tone somewhere between frantic and thankful, she said, "Thank you! Thank you for finding my niece. She was playing right beside me. The next moment, I turned around, and she was gone. I looked for her all around and was going to ask the lifeguard for help just before you got here."

Brian was mum. He just kept looking at her with a blank stare, save that his eyes seemed to be more open than usual. "I'm Katie," she said hesitantly when Brian didn't respond. "That's Isabel, my niece."

Brian just stood still, looking at her. He was smitten by her at first sight. It wasn't just her petite figure or red bathing suit. Or just her shimmering blond hair. It wasn't just her angelic voice. It was all of that. She was perfect. With a quizzical look, she turned her head and asked, "Are you okay? Are you non-verbal?"

Brian thought *non-verbal* was an odd way to say 'Are you deaf and dumb?' or 'Cat's got your tongue?'

Dave, who had followed him, looked at the two and gently punched Brian in the arm to wake him up from whatever stupor he was in. When he didn't respond to him either, he said, "Hi, Katie. I'm Dave. This is Brian. As you've seen, Brian is a hero, a saver of lost little girls." He sniggered and said, "Non-verbal. I like that. Sometimes I wish he was."

Katie smiled, extended her hand, and said, "Happy to meet you, hero."

Brian accepted her hand but didn't shake it. He just held her hand in his a bit longer than would ordinarily be customary in a greeting. "You're, ahh, you're really pretty." That's the first thing that came out of his mouth. He couldn't help it.

Katie continued to hold his hand. "Thank you. That's very sweet. You're pretty, too." Not a second later, she realized what she had just said and let go of Brian's hand, quickly stepping back. Sounding like she stuttered, she said, "I, I, mean, what I mean is, is, well, nice to, ah, meet you, Brian." She blushed a little.

Katie asked Brian and Dave to join her and Isabel on the blanket. "My friend Norma should be back in a minute. She's also looking for Isabel. I told her to come back in five if she didn't find her, and time's just about up."

Norma returned. Introductions were made. The four sat on the blanket and talked for over an hour. They realized they were all the same age and had just graduated from high school – the boys from a public school and the girls from an all-girls Catholic school. "Is what they say about girls from a Catholic school true?" asked Dave.

Norma answered, "Only half of it, but I won't tell you which half."

All shared laughter during the conversation, which was heavily peppered with innuendos. Dave and Norma got along just fine. Brian and Katie got along several notches above the *just fine* mark.

Looking at her watch, Katie said they had to leave to get Isabel back home. She wrote her phone number with her finger on patted-down sand. After giving the hand gesture of *Call me*, the group broke up, and all went their way.

Brian and Katie found they had golf in common, among several other things. Katie learned how to play from her semi-professional golfer father; Brian honed his skills while on the high school golf team during his sophomore and part of his senior year. They spent many days together playing golf and getting to know each other in many other ways.

The guys were together when Brian invited Dave to play golf with him and Katie, but rarely on other occasions. Being apart curiously brought them closer to each other as each thought about their friendship.

Brian and Katie parted at the end of summer. She went to a Catholic university in Florida; he stayed in Chicago and attended Northwestern University, as did Dave. As the weeks rolled by, Brian and Katie traded phone calls several times each week. As the months rolled by, phone calling ebbed and finally ended.

The summer spent playing golf was propitious. They took the test to join Northwestern's golf team, and both passed. Fortunately, Northwestern didn't contact Lincoln High School to get a bead on Dave and Brian's participation in their golf team.

***

Brian sat up, paused, and then stood up in the bunker. "Call the hook and ladder division at the fire department, or give me a hand out of here."

Dave extended the rake resting next to the bunker, holding it with both hands by the tines, and told Brian, "Grab the rake, you old rake."

Safely out of the bunker, Brian brushed off the sand from his legs and butt. "Get my back, won't ya?"

Dave brushed his back to flick off the sand. "Gees, Bri. Now

I'm your valet?"

Brian gave Dave a fist bump and said, "I'm glad you're good for something."

"Funny how I can forget something that happened last week but remember something that happened eons ago," said Dave.

"Remember her name? The gal on the beach?

Dave raised his eyebrows and shook his head. He changed his expression to one of surprise and said, "Tondaleya. Yeah, that was her name. Or was it Ophelia? Xena?"

Brian purposely held back his smile. "It was Katie."

"You lost your virginity to her, didn't you?"

"Hah! She lost her virginity to me."

On the green, Dave putted for a birdie. Brian putted for a par. "I'm two down from you, bud," said Dave.

"Two holes don't make a final score, Dave. Again, don't count your chickens."

They put their clubs in their bags and drove to the next hole. Dave said, "Besides you, I mean her losing her virginity status back then, I remember another thing that happened during that summer."

Brian said, "I'm all ears."

"You changed. Well, I don't mean *changed,* not in the sense that you were one thing and then another." He hummed for a second and said, "Evolved. Yeah, you evolved."

Brian put his hand on Dave's shoulder as they proceeded along the winding car path. "Dave, you're a bright guy, but you should have taken remedial speech instructions. Talk English, please."

Dave paused and thought. He wanted to make a simple point about Brian's charitable character – his penchant for helping people. If his point penetrated what he thought was Brian's thick skull, it might help Brian realize that his journey had not ended. "You liked helping people, and helping Katie back then brought you great rewards.”

”Yeah. I guess so.”

“I remember seeing some of that in you in high school. You were always there to help others. But you really drove it home on the beach. On the beach with Tondaleya.”

Brian quietly snorted. “Katie. The kid was lost. I just happened to be there. What’s the big deal?”

“The big deal is two things, bud. I’m sure many people saw that little girl crying but did nothing about it. You did. Two, it paid off. You had a great summer with Ophelia.”

“Katie. So, your point?”

Dave needed to be gentle with what he was about to say. He knew he couldn’t *tell* Brian what he should do. Brian accepted suggestions and occasionally unsolicited advice but always resisted commands. He had to feed him a thought and let him chew on it. “Here’s the skinny. You like people, and people like you. You’ve helped lots of people in the past, and they all benefited from it.” He waited for Brian to respond but heard nothing. He added, “Makes you feel good when you help someone, doesn’t it?”

Brian understood what Dave was saying and, more importantly, what Dave was trying to do. He appreciated his caring and wanting to help a friend but couldn’t wrap his mind around the notion of moving on with his life. “I’m not there, Dave.”

“Well, maybe not there right now. But it’s something to think about, no?”

“Hmm.” Brian sat quietly for the next minute. As the golf car swerved around the car path’s curves, so did Brian’s thoughts about life.

Chapter 6:

Beautiful Teeth

Except for the birds chirping in the trees and the geese chattering as they fed on the grass, the ride between holes was uneventful, tranquil, and quiet.

Neither one talked. Both were in thought. Brian thought about his laundry list of *to-dos* before he returned to Seattle. *Portfolio beneficiary, Charlotte's graphic design business, stuff sold, stuff that needed selling, the Trust, life insurance, DNR.*

Dave thought about what he could say to Brian, how to say it, and when. He held a tray of thoughts above his head, like a waiter carrying dinner to be served. If not properly balanced, all would crash on the floor and be useless. "Good, a restroom. Need to pee." Dave got out of his golf car and went inside the men's room – not to pee, but to call Nicole. He needed to vent and hoped Nicole would give him some encouraging words.

"Hope everything comes out okay," said Brian, not realizing that his funny little statement had a different meaning for Dave.

"Hi, babe. Glad I caught you. We just finished the second hole. It's grueling."

Nicole thought he was talking about the Palms Golf Course, not his dealing with Brian. "You should have played at our club."

Nicole's misunderstanding of what was 'grueling' immediately lightened Dave's problems with Brian. He guffawed and said, "Thanks. You already helped."

"Huh?"

"Never mind. Here's the thing. I'm following my plan, trying to inject Bri with encouraging words without him feeling the needle's jab."

"Sometimes, hon, someone has to feel the needle to know they're getting some good medicine."

"Hold on. I gotta flush."

"You're in the toilet?"

"In more ways than one."

Brian pounded on the men's room door. "Yo! You okay in there?"

Whispering, Dave said, "Gotta go. Bye." Louder, he said, "Yep, just washing up."

Back in the golf car, they continued their travel to the third hole. The beverage car pulled up next to them. An attractive young gal smiled and said, "Need anything, gentlemen?"

Seeing her name tag, Dave said, "No. Not now, Sharon. I'm fine. Bri?"

Brian looked at Sharon. She smiled at him. He smiled back and said, "Beautiful!"

"Sorry. I didn't hear what you wanted. Say again," she said.

"I was talking about your teeth. They're beautiful."

The beverage car gal gave him one of those *Huh?* looks when she slightly tipped her head backward and raised her eyebrows. "Oookay. Thank you. Can I get you something to eat or drink?"

"You probably floss. Right?"

Looking away from Brian, she fidgeted with her notepad and pen resting on her passenger seat. She thought it was the weirdest question she ever heard, but she didn't want to question why he questioned her. She held her own and did her job. "Yes, I do. I'll check in with you later to see if you need anything." She waved *see-ya,* said, "Have a good round," and drove off.

"That was weird, Bri. Do you floss? She must think you're a looney."

"Remember how you said you're able to remember things from years and years ago?"

"Yeah."

"I just did. When I saw her teeth…you know dentists first look at teeth when they meet someone. Well, anyway, that pretty little gal made me remember what I said…let me think…yeah, in 1976."

"Hop in. There's a twosome behind us. Or do you want them to play through?"

"Yeah, pull over. Let's wave them through. I'm in the mood to reminisce."

Dave was elated that Brian wanted to relive and perhaps feel the good things about his past.

***

His bare feet rested on the coffee table as he sat on the comfy couch reading about various periodontal diseases. Next to him were strewn other textbooks, all about dentistry, all with Post-it notes sticking out from the pages to remind himself to reread those pages.

His roommate, Chuck, sat on his desk chair reading various articles on the computer monitor about chemical engineering. Both had a passion and a drive to succeed in their respective professions. Aside from sharing a small two-bedroom apartment to keep living costs down, Brian and Chuck had little in common. Unencumbered by any need for conviviality, their economic arrangement suited them perfectly.

After finishing his evening reading, Brian clicked on the TV to catch up on Chicago and national news. As he waited for the video and sound to respond, he glanced at the framed *Bachelor of Science* diploma above the TV for the last three years and the empty frame beside it. He thought *I'll be filling you with a DDS certificate soon,*

He half-heard the news as his eyelids closed. The next sound he heard was Chuck barking at him. "Yo. It's morning. Seven. Coffee's made. See ya later."

He rose from the couch and said, "Mission accomplished. I don't have to waste time making the bed."

After his morning ritual of showering, five-minute dental care, dressing, and a very light breakfast, he wheeled his bike down two flights of steps and peddled for five miles to the dental college. Upon arrival, he tossed his coat, shirt, pants, and shoes into his locker, slipped his feet into Crocs, donned his scrubs, and walked to the reception area. "Good morning, Sally. What do you have for me today?"

Sally handed him Charlotte Hayes' patient registration form. He thumbed through it, didn't see anything remarkable, and called out to the dozen people waiting. "Ms. Hayes. Charlotte Hayes."

Charlotte rose from her chair, waved, and walked toward him. He didn't notice her comely appearance and feminine gait and signaled her to follow him to his dental chair. He was called away by one of his teachers before he arrived at his chair and, again with a wave, signaled her to have a seat. He half turned to her and said, "I'll be right back."

His face froze when he returned to his chair where Charlotte sat comfortably, at ease, and smiling, just like he had done years earlier when he had met Katie on the beach.

"Doctor?" she said.

His eyes smothered her face. With a soft, gentle tone, he said, "Beautiful!"

She saw his name tag and said, "Well, thank you, Doctor Saddle."

Brian's laugh sounded more like a giggle. He looked down at

his name tag. A fold on his scrubs partially covered it. Brushing his hand across the tag to reveal his full name, he said. "Oh, my name. Ahh, my name tag. Yeah, it's Saddlemeyer. Brian Saddlemeyer." He couldn't say more. He became a tad flush as he looked at the most beautiful woman he ever saw, live, sitting right in front of him. Feeling like an embarrassed oaf, the only words he could think to say were, "I meant beautiful teeth."

He needed to take his foot out of his mouth. "You too. I mean, you do have beautiful teeth, and, ah, you are also beautiful; I mean, shit! I don't know what I mean. Do you floss?"

Her laugh was full of understanding. She laughed *with* him, not *at* him. She extended her hand, offering a handshake. He accepted. "Happy to meet you, Doctor."

"Actually, doctor-to-be. For now, it's Brian."

"Charlotte."

"Of all the dental schools in all the towns in all the world, you walked into mine."

"Casablanca. Bogie."

Brian's smile could not have been bigger. He didn't let go of her hand, nor did she his. "Yeah, Bogie."

"You also have beautiful teeth," she said.

Brian finished his examination and called his instructor to his station to approve his diagnosis and recommendations for the patient. Brian was pleased with Dr. Erickson's check marks on Charlotte's chart and his comment: "Good job, Saddlemeyer."

"Whew!" said Charlotte. "I was worried he would say, 'Rotten teeth, yank 'em out, give her dentures.'"

Brian laughed as he adjusted the chair from its reclined position so Charlotte could sit up. He took a deep breath and exhaled. "I have bad news and good news."

With a somewhat concerned expression, she said, "Your

teacher said, '*Good job,*' so what's the bad news?"

Smiling, he said, "The bad news is that I haven't found anything that needs fixing. You don't have to come back here for another year."

"That's not bad news. It's good news."

"Yeah, good for you, but bad for me."

"Say what?"

"I won't be here next year to see you again."

Charlotte blushed. She did not mistake his words. "So, you have bad news for you and good news for me. Right?"

"Ah-huh."

The chit-chat paused for several seconds as they stared into each other's eyes.

"But if you're not here next year, you'll be a dentist, not a dental student. Isn't that good news?"

"That's called future good news. I prefer present good news."

"Everyone does, I guess."

"The present good news is that I'm not going to eat alone tonight. I thought I was going to be alone. Well, not alone. I have a roommate, a guy, but we don't talk much."

Charlotte gave him a look that was a combination of surprise, confusion, and an invitation for Brian to explain what he meant.

He asked, "Would you like to have dinner with me tonight?"

"You didn't ask if I was married or if I had a boyfriend."

Brian cleared his throat. "No, you're right. I'm certainly not a gentleman. Are you married, or do you have a boyfriend?"

She showed her beautiful teeth with a smile that penetrated Brian's heart – a smile that would live in him for the rest of his days. "Yes," she said.

He grimaced and said, "That's one *yes* for three questions. If I were a gambling man, I'd bet you answered my first question, right?"

She nodded. He smiled. "The answer to your two other questions is…well, it's a long story that I'll tell you tonight."

At day's end, Brian and Charlotte rendezvoused at Chez Laurent. Although pricier than his food budget allowed, he wanted a romantic setting for their get-to-know. He would have chosen Applebee's if he knew that Charlotte was more interested in words and feelings than atmosphere and luxury.

He arrived well before she did, sat at the table-for-two, and glanced at the entry door every five seconds. The flickering electric candle on the table mesmerized him as he thought of what to say, what to ask, and how to act. He saw his meeting with Charlotte as an interview, a chance to impress her without being overbearing, a chance to become part of her life. He made sure he took charge of all of his faculties so he wouldn't be the phumphering nerd he was, when he first met her.

She arrived. The receptionist pointed to his table. She nodded and went to him. As she walked, light beams danced on her shimmering red dress and cast a mild glow on her lovely face. Her walk resembled a runway model, causing her long, silken hair to sway. That was the first time he saw all of her, not just her face. His smile was directed at her, to show her he was happy to see her. It was also a reaction to his hormones.

He rose, waved to her, and extended his hands, thinking it would be more romantic than a handshake and less forward than a hug. She hugged him, not to be forward or to send any signal other than *Nice to see you*. She believed hugs immediately tell someone you like them, trust them, and want to be part of their life.

Charlotte didn't change one iota from the woman she was in his dental chair. She kept her friendly and enchanting demeanor and continued to fill his heart without trying.

They talked about their upbringing, jobs, desires, and hopes for all tomorrows.

He learned that she was a graphic artist, gainfully employed, with aspirations of starting her own graphics company. She was one year younger than Brian and, like him, grew up with wonderful supporting parents in a middle-income home. She never married but had a long-standing relationship with her beau until he returned to Venezuela to join his father's oil company to become a millionaire.

She said, "Yup, becoming a millionaire became more important than little ole me." She sipped chardonnay and said, "Had I known how shallow he was, we never would have been a couple. You're not shallow, are you, Bri? Do you want to become a millionaire?"

He reached across the table and placed his hand on hers. "Money is important. And sure, I'd like to be a millionaire. But money is secondary. I can't judge your ex, but I would guess that few people will be at his funeral when he dies, and fewer will say anything about his charity or soul."

"Whew. That's a mouthful. I would have settled for *No, I'm not shallow.*"

"Did I overdo it?"

She laid her hands on the table, palms upward. He responded by placing his hands on hers. Her thumbs pressed gently on his hands as she said, "No, not at all. I agree with you. For whatever reason, I don't understand right now, but I trust you. I sense that you're an honest person. A caring person."

She chuckled to lighten her words and continued, "You're also a person who should eat his beef bourguignon before it gets cold."

Their conversation continued as they ate. They filled their bellies with tasty food and their minds with delicious thoughts about being together and perhaps being together for the rest of their lives. During dessert, Charlotte said, "I have a confession, Bri. I'm transgender.”

“I don’t care,” he said. “Man, this crème brulée is great!”

She cleared her throat and said, “I don’t have a naval.”

He wiped a bit of his dessert from his lips and said, “Belly buttons are overrated. After nine months, you should get rid of them anyway.”

She smiled. Her eyes lit. “Another confession,” said Charlotte. That Venezuelan oil guy I was with? He's six feet under. I poisoned him.”

With a nonchalant shrug, he said, “I don’t care. And if I do become a millionaire, I’m going to hire the chef to be my full-time cook.”

“I have two confessions you *will* care about,” she whispered.

Brian cleared his throat, sat more erect, and said, “Go for it.”

“First, I’ve learned that if I don’t say what I’m feeling, if I don’t say what I need to say, it just doesn’t serve me well.”

“Yeah, I get that. Same here. But I do regret some of the things I’ve said, even though I needed to say them at the time.”

Charlotte delicately cleared her throat. “So far, we’re on the same page. So here’s number two.”

Brian was apprehensive about what Charlotte would say yet anxious to know what was on her mind. She leaned forward and said, “I like you. Maybe more than like. I care for you.”

“Ditto.”

“Ditto? You sound like Patrick Swayze in ‘Ghost.’”

“Huh?”

“Never mind. Not important. Let’s stick with ditto.”

“You’re right. Pretty lame. Let me define ditto. I like you too. I like you very much. Something tells me it’s even more than very much. And I care for you. A lot.”

They both smiled. They felt together as if they’d known each other for many years.

"Do you believe in love at first sight?"

"Not really," she said. "First sight says you're in love with a person's looks, not what's inside them. I believe love happens when you see into a person's soul. When you emotionally touch them, and they touch you."

"So, how does your touch feel?"

"I need to touch more before I can wrap my head around my feelings."

"So, it's not the crème brulée that does that?"

She appreciated that he lightened the conversation. "Yeah. I guess it is the dessert." Her eyes and smile exuded her true feelings, and Brian knew…he felt… that her feelings mirrored his.

The waiter asked if there would be anything else. Brain said, "No. I have everything I need, and I think the lady does too." She nodded.

After paying with cash, they left, hand in hand, and heart in heart.

***

Dave saw the twosome that played through tee off and drive down the fairway to their balls. He looked at Brian, who looked like he was in a coma. He nudged him with his elbow to get him back to consciousness and said, "Hey, bud. Get up. We're up."

Brian opened his eyes. He had a glazed look on his face as if he just awakened from a dream. "Like it was yesterday, Dave."

"Say again."

Brian told him what he had been thinking about and the memories that were still alive in him. Dave said, "I know what you mean. I remember the first time I met Nicole. If you had the same feelings about Charlotte back then as I had with Nicole, you're a lucky fellow indeed."

With an angry slant, Brian said, "Step on it. Let's play golf. I want to hit something. Hit it very hard."

Dave understood Brian's need to hit something, lash out, and get the anger out of his system by transplanting it to an inanimate object. "Here we go, bud. Hole #3 awaits us."

Chapter 7:

The Attempt and Fourth Leg

Dave pulled up to the ball washer at the third hole. He pumped the washer handle hard and fast, many more times than needed to clean his ball. As he pumped, he fantasized about a futuristic device that could wash a brain – get rid of the debris in his memory banks. He glanced at Brian, who remained in the car, mumbling inaudibly.

"Yo, Bri. We're up."

"Not from what I can see. Those guys we let play through haven't taken their fairway shot yet."

Dave looked out and saw the two guys walking around the fairway almost in circles. Something delayed their play. "Maybe they lost their ball or had to take a leak, Bri."

"Bullshit! There are no restrooms around here."

"Okay, lost ball," said Dave.

"How the hell long does it take to take a piss?"

Dave knew Brian had heard him say *lost ball* but didn't want to pounce on him for ignoring the possible reason why the golfers were walking around. "Good question. Maybe they're particular about which tree they'll use for cover."

Brian got out of the car, grabbed his 5-wood, and walked toward the two players on the fairway.

Dave called out, "Bri." And then louder: "Bri! What the hell are you doing?"

Brian didn't answer. He kept walking, swinging his club like a baseball player warming up at home plate. Dave became concerned, hopped into the car, and drove to Brian. He stopped in front of him to cut him off from going further.

"You're kidding. Are you actually going to call them out for slow play?"

"No, Dave. I'm not going to say a word. I'm just going to hit their balls for them, and I'm sure they'll get the message."

He started to walk around the car. Dave jumped out, grabbed his arm, and said, "Doctor Saddlemeyer, you're wanted in the waiting room." He continued to hold Brian's arm until he felt it relax. Brian's angry stare at the two golfers who were fifty yards out also softened. The golfers waved to Dave and Brian. One of them yelled, "Sorry. We lost a club, and it took a while to find it."

Dave waved back and yelled out, "No prob."

"Wanna play through? We'll step aside," said one of the golfers.

Dave yelled back to them, "It's okay. No rush here."

Dave let Brian cool off on the drive back to the tee box. He was beside himself with Brian's outburst, and the anger he showed added to Dave's challenge of trying to help his friend overcome depression. When they arrived at the tee box, Dave decided to call Nicole for some advice. "I'm supposed to call Nicole before she sets off on a mountain hike with the kids. I'll be right back."

Dave walked to a shady spot under a giant tree near the tee box. "Nicole, glad I got you. I have a problem and need your input."

"Of course. Shoot."

Dave reminded Nicole of their research on the typical five-step grieving process. They agreed Brian went through the denial phase, then anger, some bargaining, and was currently depressed. They decided that Brian's depressed state lasted much longer than they thought it should, and getting Brian down to Arizona might be the kick in the ass he needed.

"Either we got things backward on the grieving process, or Brian is going in reverse." Dave quickly told Nicole of their confrontation with a couple of golfers and Brian's immediate reaction to the situation.

"I think it's more of a hiccup than a phase. He's not going backward. He's just not himself these days. Don't dwell on it, honey. Stick to the plan."

Dave agreed with Nicole's take and put the matter to rest. He walked away from the shade into the sunlight and got ready to tee off. He looked at the fairway and said, "Clear sailing, Bri."

"Yeah, I can't see those suckers, so they must be off the green. Things okay with Nicole?"

Brian's words and tone told Dave that Nicole was right: it was a hiccup. Nevertheless, Dave thought it prudent to close the anger issue. "You got pissed, didn't you?"

"Yup. Don't know why. Well, you know. I'm not myself lately. I don't know how you put up with me anymore."

Dave smiled and said, "I don't know either. Maybe it's because you're my best friend."

'Balance' popped into Dave's head. *The guy's off balance.* That led to another pop: Frank Lloyd Wright. The speeding locomotive of pops led to the book report he wrote in high school. He told Brian that Wright created a three-legged chair, stating that if you had good posture, you would be stable and would not tip over; if you didn't, you would be off balance and probably fall. He told Brian he was living his life on a three-legged chair, and his balance was off. Dave offered to be Brian's fourth leg until he regained his posture.

Dave's simple statement had a significant impact on Brian. He put his hand on Dave's shoulder, squeezing it gently and shaking it. He took his sunglasses off and stared at Dave. His drooping eyelids, downcast eyes, and frown signaled his sadness. Dave was more than touched by Brian's gestures and looks. "Yeah, Dave, you're my best friend. You have been for most of my life."

Dave saw an opening in Brian's emotional armor. "How can I help you, Bri? What can I do?"

"You know why I agreed to come here, right?"

"Yeah. Because I told you I wanted to review your portfolio and give you some news."

Brian pointed his driver towards the pond adjacent to the fairway and said, "See those ducks over there? They're all in a row."

"Ducks do that. So?"

"Ducks in a row, Dave. I want to get all my ducks in a row."

"You're making me nervous, Bri. In fact, I am beyond nervous. I know what you tried to do once, and I don't want to bring it up again, but what are you talking about? Are you serious? What the hell, Bri!"

Brian again regretted what he had said. He understood why Dave was trying to cheer him up, to tell him how great his life could be, but he didn't have an appetite for Dave's words. Brian's thoughts about death took priority over thoughts about living. As luck would have it, the beverage car approached the tee box. He signaled the car gal to stop to deflect Dave's question.

"Be right back. Want anything?"

"You could say that again."

He walked to the beverage car to end the conversation about his motives for being with Dave. It was a different driver than the one who drove away when he asked her about flossing.

Dave stood at the tee box, watching Brian. *Another attempt?* he thought. He recalled what Brian's son, Tom, told him about his dad's attempt to commit suicide. Tom thought he wasn't one hundred percent committed to suicide. "If he were," as Tom said, "he would have been successful. He's a careful planner. Plans out everything. 'Mistake' is not in my dad's vocabulary. Botching a suicide attempt could not have been accidental."

Taking those words at face value, Dave needed to determine Brian's plan. Was it a plan to end his life or a strategy to move on? He needed to be convinced Brian wouldn't try it again, but if he did, he needed to know Brian's plan.

***

Brian walked around his house, tidying up whatever was out of place. He ran his hand across the bedspread, straightened the throw pillows that Charlotte loved, and said, "Perfect." He scanned the meds in his medicine cabinet, chose three, tossed all the pills into a Ziploc bag, and neatly replaced the empty containers on the shelf.

At his desk, he took a long, deep breath, wrote a note, put it in an envelope, wrote 'Tom' on it, and placed it on the fireplace mantle in front of the photograph of Charlotte holding Tom as a baby. It was one of Brian's favorite photos. If *Mother and child* needed to be defined, looking at Charlotte holding Tom would be the perfect definition. He held the frame as if he was holding Charlotte's face. "It's time," he said. "It's best."

The drive to the cemetery on that Friday morning was without incident. He drove carefully so a cop wouldn't stop him. Tears rolled down his cheeks as he recalled many memories. He spoke out to the non-existent passenger in his car as if he had been sent back in time and was reliving the happenings. He gently hit his brake when he saw an elderly man and woman walking hand-in-hand, looking into storefronts. The *Honk!* from the pickup truck behind him put him back on his drive.

The cemetery's ornate iron entry gate opened slowly. It gave him pause to change his mind but didn't sway him from his plan. He drove to Charlotte's gravesite every Sunday for the last three months. *Not this time,* he thought. *Better to leave the car in the parking lot. It won't block the street next to her grave.* Out loud, he said, "Why the hell do I care where my car is parked?" His head spun while anger and sadness took turns controlling his emotions. He drove on.

At the gravesite, Brian knelt in front of Charlotte's tombstone. He placed his hand on it, bowed his head, and spoke to her. "I know you know I am here. I can feel you." His emotions welled up, and his body shivered. "Soon, love, we'll be together."

He took the Ziploc bag out of his pocket and realized he didn't bring any water. He tossed all the pills into his mouth. Crunching on them like mixed nuts, he laid down on the grass, looking up to the heavens. He closed his eyes. Sleep was approaching. Permanent sleep was imminent.

***

Brian had left the house just moments before Tom arrived for his visit. Tom knocked on the door and rang the bell, but his father didn't answer. He took the key hidden behind the porch light, unlocked the door, and yelled, "Dad! Hey, Dad. It's me." Tom walked around the house, continuing to call out. He looked out at the back patio, pool, and garage. *No car. Hmm,* he thought. He phoned him but only got a *Please leave a message* response.

He grabbed a beer from the fridge and went into the family room to watch TV while he waited for his father to return. He scrolled through the program guide on the TV, not caring much about what was listed. He clicked the remote, and a news program came on. He wanted to stay informed about national and global events but found "news" favored negative stuff more than positive events and decided to search for something uplifting. He spoke to the TV as if it was asking him questions while he read the guide. "No. Nope. Definitely no." And so it went until a golf tournament popped up. He clicked on it. A commercial was airing. He sat down and quickly sprung up when he saw the envelope on the mantle. He had an immediate gut reaction. "Shit!"

He read his father's note, his goodbye, his words of love. His mind raced with questions about where his father might have gone. Rereading his father's last words, he knew where his father was. As if his dad was in the room, he spoke to him: "You're with mom. I know you are."

Tom raced to the cemetery, not caring about red lights, stop signs, or his speed. He arrived at his mother's gravesite five minutes after Brian had arrived. He ran to his father, who was lying on the grass motionless, calling, "Dad! Dad!"

He knelt and checked his vitals, discovering that he had a weak pulse and was breathing, although shallowly. He saw powder residue on his dad's lips and his tongue hanging limply in his open mouth. He noticed his dad's clenched fist holding a clear plastic bag with a few pills in it.

He whipped out his phone and called 911. "I'm at St. Mathew's Cemetery. My father took poison. Pills. He's still alive. He's sixty-nine. Trace my location, and please hurry."

Tom knew CPR wasn't necessary while his father kept breathing and his heart was pumping blood, but he thought any helpful action was better than inaction. He pressed on his chest five times and then leaned closer to exhale into his dad's mouth. *What am I doing? CPR isn't called for. Where the hell is the ambulance?* "You're going to be okay, Dad. I promise."

Miraculously, an ambulance arrived minutes later. Paramedics took over from Tom and proceeded to follow their protocols.

"I'm a doctor," said Tom to the EMTs. What can I do?"

"Just step aside, doc. We got it from here."

Tom stepped aside so the EMTs could perform their magic.

With an oxygen mask on and a saline solution dripping into his father's vein, the EMTs wheeled the gurney into the ambulance.

Tom followed them to the hospital. In the ER, staffers quickly did what they did best: they saved Brian Saddlemeyer's life.

Knowing his father was in good hands, Tom phoned his wife to tell her he would stay in Seattle until his dad was out of the hospital. He then called Dave, who said he would be in Seattle the next day. Brian gained consciousness an hour later. Tom told him that Dave would be coming the next day. "Please call Dave, Tom. Tell him I'm fine. Tell him I was an idiot, but now I'm okay. Tell him he doesn't need to be here. Everything's okay."

***

Balancing a beverage in each hand, Brian strolled back from the beverage car, his face illuminated with a satisfied grin. He handed one to Dave and said, "Bloody Mary. Too early for a bloody beer."

Seeing a smile on Brian's face was more refreshing than the thought of drinking a Bloody Mary. Wanting to reinforce the feeling he had about Brian's feelings, Dave retorted, "Bloody good, chap. Thanks."

"What I meant about my last game of golf is that my joints aren't what they used to be. I'm always in pain when I play, so I decided to give up golf."

Dave was skeptical, sensing an underlying issue. He wanted to confront the issue aggressively but wasn't sure it was the right time. To pursue what Brian meant, he would have to do so gently. He took the Bloody Mary from Brian and said, "Okay then. You had me worried there for a minute."

"Yeah, I know. Sorry. Don't worry."

"Ducks in a row, Bri?"

"Oh, yeah. I meant I wanted to review all of my documents and portfolio, like you said. I think it's about time I paid attention to that, you know, just to, well, pay attention to it. I haven't done anything about anything for a year. I mean anything financial. I'm babbling. You said you wanted to do that too and had some news for me."

Again, Dave wanted to believe what Brian had told him but found what he had said questionable. Dave danced on emotional cinders, fearing they could flame up any second.

"We'll talk after you tee off."

Chapter 8:

Friends Help Friends

Brian gave himself an emotional slap in the face for his slips of the tongue. He needed to accomplish his plan, to make sure the transfer of his holdings passed fluidly to his son and sister-in-law and for his best friend to accept his goodbye. He needed to stay on track, be the friend Dave knew, and not act like he needed psychiatric help.

They stood on the tee box at Hole #3. Brian took a few practice swings but wasn't thinking about hitting his ball. He thought of a simple way to relax Dave, to get Dave off his back with his suggestions and advice about moving on in life. *Tell a joke.*

"Wahoo!" said Brian. "That's the best shot I had on this hole today." He looked at Dave, hoping he got the joke.

It worked. With a smile, Dave said, "Good one. Both the drive and the funny line. Straight and far, Bri."

"My joke was straight and far, or my drive?"

"Both, I guess. My turn. Don't forget to pick up your tee. You know they cost about five cents each."

"Whew, thanks," said Brian. You just saved me a nickel."

Dave knew better than to think about something other than his golf swing when he teed off. The *other* was Brian's sullen behavior and thoughts about what to say to him and how to help his friend. He liked that Brian told a joke but anticipated that the other shoe would drop the next time Brian spoke. He couldn't shake the thought that Brian was like the ball in a pinball machine, bouncing uncontrollably this way and that depending on the words he heard or the memories he recalled. Distraction is not a golfer's friend. His drive was errant, fading to the right toward a fairway bunker.

Brian heard Dave say, "Shit!" He wanted to continue with his plan to put Dave at ease. *Another joke,* he thought.

"Dave, did I ever tell you about the monster bunker I landed in but got out of it with ease?"

"Nope. Where? When?"

Brian recounted a game he played a few years ago. "I walked into a bunker and looked at my lie. It was at the bottom of the highest side of the bunker. I was facing a tsunami-like wall of sand."

"What did you do to get out?"

"I followed the footsteps I made when I walked into the bunker and walked out with ease. Archie Bunker gave me that advice."

Dave appreciated the joke even though it was a groaner. "And your ball?"

"Well, it cost more than a nickel, so I raked it out. Took a double bogey, which I thought was fair, and kissed the hole goodbye."

"The folks you played with said a double was enough?"

"I was playing with Erickson. His favorite golf phrase was *It's a gimmie,* so he didn't much care about what score I took."

Dave got in the golf car to drive to his ball, thinking about what to do with this guy he wanted to help who had shunned all help. He was slightly put at ease when he heard Brian's groaner. He thought, *Shut up and listen? Knock some sense into him? Give him an opening to open up?* He didn't have an answer but wanted Brian to keep talking, hoping he would say something to allow Dave to pivot and discuss Brian's future. "Do you still keep in touch with Erickson?"

The question hung in the air, embodying Dave's eagerness to explore the present and the ties that bound them to the past. "Pull over into the shade. No one's behind us. I'll tell you about Adam."

***

Several months before Brian received his DDS, Adam Erickson moved to Seattle and bought a small dental practice. Erickson offered Brian a junior partnership at his practice the day after graduation.

"I'm the only dentist here. I want to expand the practice and need a good partner, especially one with a baccalaureate in business." He continued with a broad, purposely artificial smile: "The fact that I like you has nothing to do with it."

"Wow," he replied. "I've been offered the president's job at UI Dentistry and a sorter at Amazon's plant, so I'll have to think about it, doctor."

"Adam."

"Right. Adam. Seattle? Lots of rain in Seattle, no?"

Erickson laughed. "Okay, you convinced me. I'll buy you an umbrella."

Brian laughed. "Yeah, dumb question. I truly am honored, doc…Adam, but I need to think about it. Have to talk to my better half. Hold on."

"Sure."

No sooner did Brian hear *sure* when he said, "Okay, I thought about it. I accept your offer even though I don't even know the whole offer."

"And your better half?"

Coincidentally, Charlotte's sister, Peggy, moved to Seattle a year earlier. Brian guessed Charlotte would go for the idea, but if she didn't, Brian could always change his mind. His guess was right.

He called Adam later that day. "Adam. Brian. I still accept your offer, but let's work out the details late next month after I return from my honeymoon in Hawaii."

"Great," said Erickson. See ya soon."

Hugs, kisses, and joyous welcomes were given to the

newlyweds when they arrived at Peggy's house in mid-July. Their meticulous plan was panning out. Remaining was finding a permanent place to live and setting up Charlotte in her new business as a graphic designer. Charlotte ribbed Brian for keeping a checklist of everything they needed to do but entirely accepted that Brian was a *Cross the Ts and Dot the Is* guy.

Their first few days with Peggy and her husband were spent touring the Seattle sights and scouting for rental apartments and Charlotte's studio space. To their delight, they found an apartment – not luxurious, but in good shape – not in the neighborhood they wanted, but one that seemed to have a community spirit. The cherry on top was that a small store near their apartment was available for a lease. It was the perfect size for Charlotte's business. All was proceeding exceedingly well.

Charlotte's first client was Sundance Dental, the practice owned by Erickson and his new junior partner, Brian. The mailers and the website she created for them caught the attention of several other businesses, and her company, Crown Graphics, was off and running in no time.

Two years into co-running Sundance Dental, Brian approached Erickson with a forward-thinking proposal. "There are lots of dental offices in Seattle, and there are many specialists. Orthos, perios, pediatric care…well, just about everything a set of teeth could need."

"Yup. We know lots of them. Recommended many of them to our patients. So?"

"Why don't *we* have all of the specialists here? Well, not here in this office, but in a bigger one. Why don't we start an all-services clinic, maybe a dental hospital?"

Erickson rocked back and forth on his desk chair. He stopped, leaned forward, and said, "Great idea. I like it. But I doubt we can convince the specialists to join us. They're probably making a bundle sitting pretty in their practices. And then there's the question of financing it."

"I agree, Adam. We don't ask the veterans to join us. We recruit new people."

"New people?"

Brian was visibly excited that his partner seemed open to the idea. All he needed to do was lay out his plan. "You hired me right out of school. How about we do the same thing and get an orthodontist to join us? Then a periodontist and so on?"

Erickson went back to rocking. He tapped his lower lip with his pen a few times, leaned forward, and said, "Money?"

Brian guffawed. "Got that covered. My best friend, Dave Sherman, is a financial whiz. He put the whole thing together for us. All we have to do is sign for a small business loan. We'll have enough for recruitment and leasing a bigger office."

Erickson stood up and extended his hand to Brian. "I have to pat myself on the back for my brilliance in hiring a dentist who knew a thing or two about business. Let's do it."

Time swiftly unfolded, witnessing the evolution of Sundance Dental. Brian's proposal to secure full partnership found a willing acceptance from Erickson. Dental specialists, hygienists, and clerical staff were hired, occupying their new colossal office space. Sundance became the only dental practice in Seattle that offered one-stop-shopping for any dental needs. Prosperity followed.

Needing to fill his coffers to pay for his extracurricular activities, Erickson suggested that Brian become the majority shareholder in the clinic. Not wanting to delve into Erickson's private affairs and wanting to help Erickson in any way he could, he paid Erickson a tidy sum without question and became seventy-five percent owner of the clinic.

Brian's dedication and initiative paid off. He lived a carefree and comfortable life – the American dream. He was happily married, had a wonderful son who became a prominent physician and was financially sound.

He and Charlotte sold their businesses when Brian turned sixty. The first notation on their bucket list was to travel the world. The year they spent doing so was glorious.

"What have I done to deserve all of this? A beautiful and loving wife, a fabulous son, and a career that gave me enjoyment almost every day."

"Whew, Brian. I don't know," said Charlotte, wrapping her arms around him. "I'll need a thesaurus to find all the words I could use, like love, charity, honesty, industry___"

"Okay, okay. The only word I can think of is *you*. If not for you, my life would not be this life. It wouldn't even be close."

***

"It wouldn't even be close," said Brian.

"Huh?" asked Dave.

Brian sipped the last of his Bloody Mary. "Sorry. I was thinking about Adam and the dental practice we built, which led me to think about Charlotte."

"I'll bite," said Dave. "What wouldn't even be close?"

"Forget it. Not important. You asked about Adam. Well, he took a turn for the worse."

"Medical thing?"

"Yeah, you could say that." Brian stared at Dave and tapped his finger on his forehead.

Dave's eyes lit up. "No. Mental illness? Schizophrenia? Something like that?"

"Humph!" uttered Brian. "I think the best words to describe what happened are infidelity and stupidity. Throw in dishonesty, lack of respect, and fear for good measure. Is there a medical condition for all of that?"

Dave was intrigued by what Brian said. Possibilities of what happened to Erickson flitted across his mind. He was anxious to know but didn't know if Brian wanted to tell him. Deciding that the best reaction to what Brian said was no reaction, he sat quietly and waited for Brian to speak. Five seconds felt like minutes to Dave until Brian told him the story about Erickson.

"Adam was a devoted husband. No man I know…well, besides you and me…loved their wife more and would give their life for her. So it seemed."

Brian stopped talking. His eyeballs danced as he recalled memories. He wasn't sure about what to tell Dave about Erickson.

"I guess I can chalk it up to hormones. Every man I know has a fantasy now and then. You know, you see a beautiful woman, and testosterone flows from your crotch to your brain. That's happened to me. Before Charlotte was in my life, I didn't turn the faucet off." Brian started to laugh.

"What's funny about turning your faucet off?" asked Dave.

"Ha. Just had a wild vision of testosterone dripping from a kitchen faucet." He kept his smile and shook his head. "It's a pearlescent blue."

"What is?"

"Testosterone." His guffaw told Dave that he liked his sick take.

"Okay, weirdo. Get back to the story."

Brian cleared his throat and erased the faucet image. "So, while I was married to Charlotte, turning the faucet off was easy. Got to the point where the faucet just stayed off."

The faucet controlling Dave's anxiety level turned on. "My guess is that he had an affair. Right?"

"And then some."

"More than one affair?"

"No, just one. Just one that I know about."

"So what's the *then some*?"

Brian recounted what Erickson told him about one of his dental patients, Sylvia. "I didn't meet her when she was at our office, but I do remember seeing her in his chair. You know how you do a double take when you pass by a beautiful woman?"

Dave nodded and said, "In my youth, yeah. Get back to the *then some*."

"Adam told me he couldn't control himself."

"You're kidding. Right then and there, in his office?"

Brian shook his head. "No, no. No sex then and there. It was later that night. At her place."

"I'm guessing he was married at the time?"

"Yup. This was about twenty years ago. Adam and Evelyn were married for, I don't know, maybe ten years?"

"Evelyn?"

"Yeah. Evelyn. Why?"

"Adam and Eve?"

"Hmm. Maybe that's why she insisted on being called Evelyn. Anyway___ "

Dave put his fingers to his lips. "Shh. I have a vision. I see an apple."

"Now, who's the weirdo, weirdo?" asked Brian.

"Okay. The vision is over. Just one question. Was Evelyn a snake?"

Brian closed his eyes, shook his head, and said, "A snake?"

"Never mind. So what happened to Erickson?"

"A son happened."

Dave threw his body back into the backrest. "Holy shit! So what did he do?"

"The son?"

"No, you ass. Erickson."

Brian purposely smiled. His plan of relaxing Dave was working.

A golf car with a man and woman pulled up next to Brian and Dave. "Gentlemen," said the guy. "Backup delay on the fairway?"

"No, said Dave. We're just taking a break. Play through if you want."

Brian piped in: "Dave wants to know what happened to Adam and Eve."

Dave closed his eyes and bowed his head. He resisted groaning. The man scrunched his face, having no idea what Brian meant, but decided *okey dokey* was an appropriate reply and moved on to play the hole.

Dave resisted an outward smile but was happy inside that Brian was easing back to the jokester he loved. "What's with Erickson? What's with his son? Did Evelyn, a.k.a. Eve, ever find out? Please finish the story before we have dinner tonight."

Brian explained that Erickson felt obligated to help the mother of his child but couldn't be involved in rearing their son. He suppressed his emotions about having a child out of wedlock, especially while he was married, but agreed to help financially. He sent money to Sylvia every month for twenty years running.

"Got it. I think. The kid, his son, was twenty years old, and Erickson decided to stop supporting Sylvia. Right?"

"Yes, the money stopped. You should ask *why* it stopped."

Dave huffed. Sounding slightly annoyed, Dave slowly asked, "Why did he stop sending money?"

"Good question, Dave." Brian started to laugh and then became sullen. He traveled from the present conversation to memories of the past. He again gave himself an emotional slap. "Sorry. I was trying to remember what happened. You know, the sequence of events."

"Yeah, I get it. Take your time."

"He stopped sending her money because she wanted too much for the wrong reason, on top of her lie."

"Too much for the wrong reason?"

"A thousand Benjamins. Work that out, Mr. Accountant."

"She wanted $100,000? Unbelievable! For what?"

"To hire a lawyer to get her son…his son…out of jail. Seems he decided to go into the burglary business and got caught."

"So she lied about her son needing a lawyer?"

"No, that was the truth."

Dave shook his head vigorously. "$100k? Did she want to hire O.J.'s lawyer? What's his name, Johnnie Cochran?"

"Sounds that way, doesn't it? No, not Cochran. Somebody else, I guess. The $100k wasn't all for a lawyer."

"Aha, so that was the lie. She also wanted to buy a Rolls Royce, right?"

"Blackmail."

Dave was shocked. He would have slammed on the brakes if he were driving. "As in, if you don't give me the money, I'll tell your wife?"

"You got it."

There's nothing worse than hearing a story that has no ending, so Dave needed to ask, "Did she tell his wife?"

"Adam told me that he had to come up with the blackmail money in a week. I told him I would contact Sylvia to see if I could find a way to help him help her and help his son. And prevent blackmail. I went to see her that night."

"I assume she lived in Seattle."

Brian's eyes shot up. "No, Dave. She lived in Greece. I flew there on a private jet."

"Okay, that was a stupid question. What did you tell her?"

"Nothing. Didn't need to. I knocked on her door, and a guy answered. I asked him if Sylvia was at home. He said she…now get this…she *and her husband* were on vacation."

"Husband? She never told Erickson?"

"Yes, and yes."

The beverage car was approaching them. Brian waved to the driver to stop. "This storytelling makes me thirsty," said Brian. He ordered another Bloody Mary. Dave was concerned about Brian's alcohol intake but decided to keep mum.

Brian took a long sip of his drink, uttered *Ah*, and said, "There's more to the story."

"I'm holding my breath."

Brian took another sip of his drink, uttered another *ah,* and said, "Before I told him about Sylvia being married, I wanted to know more, like to whom and for how long. I hired a private investigator."

"You really went above and beyond, didn't you."

"It was worthwhile. Worthwhile back then and even now that I'm recalling all of it."

Dave's eyes opened wide as he shook his head. "Incredible. Sylvia and her husband must have been laughing all the way to the bank."

"Laughing for *fifteen years*! That's how long they were married. And my private eye guy told me something else that blew my mind."

"There is an ending to this, isn't there?"

"There is an ending. I'll get to it in good time, but for now, I want to pay you back by not telling you how it ended."

"Pay me back? For what?"

"Making me use your old clubs so you could beat me today."

Dave was frustrated by not knowing the story's ending and delighted that Brian's jokester character continued to emerge. With a serious tone, he said, "I apologize, Bri. You're right. I wanted to beat your ass by giving you loser's clubs." With a friendly tone, he raised his voice and said, "Now, will you tell me?"

"The private eye tracked down the husband. He was a prosthodontist."

"Sounds like a prostitute. What is that?

"It's no fun just telling you. I'll give you a hint. Sylvia has beautiful teeth."

"He's a dentist?"

"Yup. She needed a new crown on one of her teeth. He suggested that she see Sam Snyder. Sam was part of our practice."

"I take it Sam did crowns?"

"Yup, again. He preferred being called a prosthodontist instead of the crown guy."

"Jeez. You can't make up this kind of stuff. A dentist has an affair, and she winds up marrying the dentist she was referred to by the dentist who got her pregnant. And then she and her dentist husband rake in lots of cash from the first dentist for many years but want more money, so they threaten blackmail."

"Good synopsis, Dave. Couldn't have said it better."

Dave again shot back in his seat. "Unbelievable! How did it end?"

Brian lowered his head slightly, gazed at Dave, and said, "I was his friend. I guess I still am. I gave him some advice to help him. That's what friends do."

Dave smiled. He saw the light at the end of the tunnel. Brian's words, *That's what friends do* rang clear. It was the first time he felt that Brian was accepting what he was trying to do to help him. "Advice?"

"I didn't need to tell him what to do about Sam. He took care of that on his own. I did tell him to fess up, tell his wife that he screwed a woman, got her pregnant, and has been helping her financially for many years."

"Did he?"

"Yup."

"Turned out okay?"

"Yup. Adam and Evelyn are still married and seem to be very happy."

Dave chewed on the fascinating story for a moment and then realized how it paralleled Bria'n's situation. "Well, my friend, everyone makes mistakes, and mistakes can be remedied."

"Not everyone," said Brian.

"How about you?"

With an air of bravado, Brian said, "Nope. Haven't made any."

"But you're thinking about making one, aren't you?"

It was clear to Brian what Dave was getting at, but he didn't want to fess up or discuss his decision to join Charlotte, so he chose to divert the conversation. "Let me tell you about the kid, the twenty-year-old kid."

"In jail, out?"

"Funny you should ask."

Dave uttered a sound of exhaustion. "Is this the never-ending story?"

Brian cleared his throat several times. "You're not going to believe this. The kid, Dylan, is running for congressman in the 8th District in Seattle."

"You're kidding! Tell me you're kidding."

Brian threw out his hands and said, "Okay, I'm kidding."

"No, asshole. Don't tell me you're kidding because I asked you to. Tell me the Dylan kid is *not* running for a congressional seat."

"No, he's not. I *am* kidding. I just wanted to pull your chain. You have to remember, I'm Brian."

Chapter 9:

You Can't Change Yesterday

Dave stopped his golf car next to the tee box, got out, and retrieved his driver. Brian sat in the car, eyes closed. After a few seconds, Dave asked, "Snoozin' Bri?"

Brian jerked slightly and opened his eyes. "What the hell hole is this?"

Dave pointed his driver to the sign next to the tee box. "Unless some kids were fooling around with the signs, I think it's number four."

Sounding surprised, Brian said, "Four?"

"Yup, four."

"Call the pro shop, Dave. Get a maintenance guy out here."

Dave scrunched his face, trying to figure out why Brian asked for maintenance. He looked around but didn't see anything that needed fixing. The only guess that made sense was that Brian was pulling his leg and was about to lay on a joke. "What's the joke?"

Deadpan, Brian said, "No joke, bud." He pointed to the far side of the tee box. A goose was at the edge of the rough near a large Calliandra bush. "Dead goose."

Dave walked to the goose, clucking to excite it and have it run off. The goose didn't move. "You called it, Bri. The goose is dead. Maybe got hit by a golf ball."

"Call the pro shop!"

Guessing that Brian was serious with his request, Dave said he would right after they teed off and walked back to the tee box.

"I'm not teeing off till the goose is taken care of," said Brian.

Dave didn't know how to play the situation. On the one hand,

Brian could have been legitimately distracted by having a dead goose within eyeshot as he teed off; on the other hand, if they agreed to come, the maintenance crew would take a long time coming and delay their game. Dave said, "I'll take care of it."

"You don't have a shovel."

Dave stopped, turned around, and said, "You're serious, aren't you? You want to bury the goose?"

"It was alive, and now it's dead." Brian's knees hit the ground. His demeanor resembled actors in a movie that had just witnessed a horrendous tragedy. He was breathing heavily, fighting off tears. His plan to get Dave off his back took a detour.

It clicked. Dave realized the connection between Brian's words and Charlotte's passing. He put his hands on Brian's shoulders and tenderly said, "I know, Bri. I know."

Brian stood up and wiped his eyes with his forearm. "Sorry, Dave. It just got to me. You know?"

Dave said as tenderly as he could, "Yes, I know."

Seconds passed as both men stood on the tee box, not speaking – not needing to speak. Dave's frustration was getting the best of him. Rapid-fire thoughts self-argued: *Console him, hit him with a golf club, hug him, be direct, hit him hard with reality, shut up.*

Brian shivered and said, "Enough. Let's play."

"Bri, I can take care of the goose if you want me to. Or we can skip this hole. Up to you."

Brian swung his driver back and forth to loosen up in preparation for his drive. "I'm over it, Dave. It's a goose. It's not Charlotte. I get it. I'm fine. Let's play."

Dave was relieved yet still concerned about Brian's state of mind. Not knowing what to do or what to say he played along with Brian's bidding. "You got it."

Brian teed up his ball. He surveyed the 150-yard, par 3 fairway and thought, *What the hell. Take a chance.* He casually swung his 4-iron back and forth and huffed, "Watch this, bud."

"4-iron?" said Dave. "Isn't that a bit too much club?"

"Was twenty years ago. Now it's perfect. Three skips."

"Huh?"

"I need more club to compensate for the three skips the ball will take on the pond."

"You're nuts. Why not less club, lots of loft to clear the pond, and bingo? Maybe even a hole-in-one."

"A hole-in-one is even more spectacular if it's preceded by three skips."

"Okay, fine, but you're takin' a chance that you don't need to."

With a huff and broad smile, Brian said, "Well, bud, I'm going to take a chance. Isn't life all about taking chances?"

Dave was taken aback. Brian's comment came out of nowhere. In many ways, it was the most positive statement he made all day. It was also an excellent springboard for Dave to dive into more positive comments to help Brian get on with living.

"Aristotle was right," said Dave.

"He played golf?"

"Not sure, but he did play at defining life. He said, ___"

Brian stopped swinging his 4-iron and interrupted him. "What the hell does a guy who died before golf was invented have to do with me having some fun?"

Dave felt good that he got an opening from Brian to pursue his thoughts about life. "Look, my friend. You're going through a terrible time in your life. You're still grieving. You tried to kill yourself. You haven't had a moment of happiness since Charlotte died."

Brian was vacant of any visible emotion. Calmly, he said, "Enough. Let me take my shot."

A door opened. He had to enter. "No, Bri. I can't let it go. I love you, man. You're tearing me apart. You're tearing yourself apart. You're miserable. Is that what Charlotte wants for you?"

"I'll ask her soon enough."

Dave's anger was apparent. He forcefully threw his golf ball into the pond to alleviate his tension. "What the hell does that mean? You sound like you're going to try suicide again!"

"No, no, no, Dave. I didn't mean that. I meant I'm getting on in years. So are you, you know. We're not going to live forever. Our day will come. This day, however, I'm going to skip a ball across the pond and land on the green."

Dave didn't buy it. "Bullshit, Bri!"

Brian put his club down and grabbed Dave's shoulders. Looking him straight in the eye, he said, "I'm not bullshitting you. You're right. I've been having a shitty life lately. Sometimes, I feel I'm at the turning point. Ya know. Getting on with life. Sometimes, I don't feel that way. Being here with you is great. Now, can I take my shot?"

Dave had two thoughts: *Brian was telling the truth -- drop the conversation; Brian's covering up -- push him to uncover his thoughts.* He patted Brian's shoulder and said, "I still think you're taking a chance you don't need to take, but please don't hit that duck in the pond."

Brian swung his 4-iron. His ball skipped across the pond. One, two, three skips, and then it hit the pond's elevated edge and got stuck in the rough. "Shit," said Brian. "If maintenance cut that grass down another few inches, I would have been on."

Still tense, Dave tightly grabbed his golf club and walked onto the tee box, resisting his urge to lash out at his friend. He thought about what to do: *Don't let go—confront him. Play along with his lie. Confront him later.* "Look at the bright side, Bri. You don't have to take a penalty stroke. A chip from there and one putt gives you a par."

"That's two over a hole-in-one."

"Now *you're* the accountant. Let me show you what you should have done."

Dave teed up, elevating his ball a fraction of an inch off the grass. He swung his 6-iron and sent his ball on a high arc before it landed ten feet from the pin. On the green, Brian chipped and one putted to get a par. Dave two-putted and also got a par. They looked at each other and shrugged.

Brian said, "Golf scoring needs to change."

"Why? How?"

"It's one-sided. If you lose your ball, you're penalized a stroke. If you land in an unplayable area and have to drop your ball elsewhere so you can hit it, you're penalized a stroke."

"Yeah, that's right. You know the rules. So how is that not fair?"

"You don't get extra credit for spectacular play. If you get a par but got it because you had an impossible shot that you miraculously made, you still only have a par."

Dave let out a sigh and uttered, "Yeah, yeah. You're right. But the same unfairness happens in just about all sports, so in a sense, it's fair."

"Like what?" asked Brian.

"Basketball. Off the backboard, bounces on the rim, and then goes in versus net-only. Two points either way. Baseball."

Brian interrupted him. "Stick with basketball. Two points if you sink a shot, but it's three points if it's outside the three-point arc."

"Weak argument, Bri. The greater the distance in basketball, the greater the number of points, but in golf, the distance from tee to hole is the same for all players."

"Right back atcha, Dave. Weak argument. The distance might be the same, but water skipping a ball onto the green is harder than simply landing on the green."

Dave rolled his eyes. "You know this is a stupid conversation, don't you?"

Brian humphed. "Fine. Just lookin' to get a pat on my back for a miraculous par."

"How about I give you a little gold star that you can put on the scorecard so people know your total score was achieved after you made a miraculous shot?"

Without a smile and without looking at Dave, Brian said, "You better get a book of stars, bud."

"Good up and down," yelled a man near the green.

"Thanks," said Brian. "It's called a miraculous par. My partner here got a boring par."

Dave saw the guy raise his eyebrow in response to Brian's comment and then search the rough, probably looking for his golf ball. "Lose a ball?" Dave asked.

"Yeah, my son's. I'm teaching him how to play." He laughed, "He's teaching me how to find golf balls."

"Got it, Dad," yelled the boy. He picked up his ball and walked toward his father.

His father waved for him to stop. "You have to hit your next shot from where the ball landed. So next time, don't pick it up. For now, hold the ball knee-high and drop it."

On the one hand, Dave admired the guy for teaching his son the game's rules, not just how to hit a ball. On the other hand, Dave thought the kid should have some fun – to heck with the rules. Teach them later. "Kids," said Dave. "How old is he?"

"Ten."

"Good age to learn."

Brian said, "We were ten, weren't we, Dave?"

"A hundred years ago. Yeah, we were ten once."

"Is that when you learned how to play?" asked the guy.

"Yup, ten," said Brian. Dave disagreed but nodded in agreement.

"Have fun, bud. Teach him well. You're a good dad for doing that," said Dave.

Brian brushed the grass with his club as he casually returned to their golf car. He turned and saw the boy hit his golf shot. Smiling, he said, "Weren't we ten when we learned how to play?"

"Depends, Bri. I think you were ten when your dad introduced you to golf. I was eleven or twelve. But we learned the rules and honed our game when we were fifteen. We were in our sophomore year."

"Ha!" yelled Brian. "Yeah. That was on the high school golf team. What a kick!"

"Kick in the sense of getting kicked off the team," replied Dave as he huffed.

Brian stopped walking. With a somber expression, he said, "I want to apologize to you. Let's get in the golf car."

Dave guessed that Brian was touched by seeing a guy teaching his son. He thought Brian remembered when he taught his son how to play. Recalling that would fuel Brian's want to keep on living. He was ready to hug his best friend and give him all the consoling words he could muster. They sat quietly in the car for a few seconds until Dave said, "Thank you, Bri. You know I would do anything for you. I'm glad you're starting to open up and take a hard look at your life."

Brian's face was contorted. "Huh?" he said.

"Your apology. It's not really needed. Just know I'm here for you," said Dave.

Brian threw his head back and laughed. He talked to himself out loud. "I'm playing golf with a nut job!"

"I don't think we're on the same page, my friend," said Dave.

Brian stopped laughing. He looked at Dave with sympathetic

eyes and said, "Not only are we not on the same page, but we're also reading different books."

Dave could see his knuckles turn white as the blood left his hands while he forcefully grabbed the steering wheel. "Let's start again. What is your apology for?"

"Getting us kicked off the golf team."

***

Daryl Henning instilled in his students an appreciation of math and how it impacted everyday life. He used golf to explain angles, distance, addition, and subtraction. He was passionate about golf and took the coaching job for Lincoln, the boys' golf team.

Henning sat in the bleachers watching the Wildcats baseball team practice. He waved to his friend, fellow teacher, and baseball coach, Hank Farmer. Farmer joined him on the bleachers for a few moments of chit-chat. Henning asked, "Are there any good players who would rather play golf than baseball?"

"If they're good, they'd probably prefer baseball," said Farmer. Giving Henning a gentle elbow bump in his ribs, he said, "You know it's America's favorite sport."

"Not sure about that, but *favorite* does have a half-life."

"You lost me."

"Things lose their importance, energy, potency over time," said Henning. "Did you know that 8.6 percent of teenage boys play baseball, but less than one percent of guys over forty-five play baseball?"

"No, I didn't know that, but it makes sense. Are those the actual stats?"

With a serious tone, Henning said, "Hank, my friend, you should also know that 27.3 percent of statistics are made up on the spot."

Both of them laughed. "So what's your point, Daryl?"

"I have an opening for two kids on the golf team. If you're thinking of cutting any kids from the Wildcats, you know, the kids that are not cutting it, but you can't find it in your heart to cut them, let me know."

"What does a baseball player bring to golf?"

"The swing, Hank. The swing." Henning stood up, mimicked a stage-performing singer from the 1930s, swung his arms in the air, and sang, "It don't mean a thing if it ain't got that swing, Doo-ah, doo-ah, doo-ah."

Farmer shook his head as he shook Henning's hand. "I didn't know if you could dance or sing, but now I know."

Henning was delighted with the compliment but then realized it was vacuous. "Good one. Very PC."

"Yeah, sometimes I talk like a politician."

"Give it some thought, Hank. Do it for the kids, not for me. You know, *One for the Gipper*."

Farmer huffed. "Look, I'll talk to a couple of my guys. I'll tell them about golf if they know who the Gipper is or even heard of Knute Rockne."

Henning said, "Deal."

Dave and Brian were on the Wildcats baseball team. Both were very good batters, but fielding was not their forte. Farmer put them in the games to pinch hit and allowed them an inning or two as outfielders. He approached both of them before practice the day after he met with Henning.

"Hey, guys. Look. You're both great hitters, but you have to confess that your heart isn't into fielding. Did you ever think about golf? There are two openings at Lincoln."

Dave scrunched his face and said, "Golf?" Chagrined, with a

worried look on his face, he asked, "You kicking us off the baseball team?"

Brian jumped in: "If Dave's out, so am I."

"Let's walk," said Farmer. With his arms around their shoulders, Farmer told them he was not kicking them off the team but offering them a choice of which sport they wanted to play. He told them that not only would they learn how to play a great game, but they would also play in every game, never benched.

"Golf's for old people," said Brian.

Laughing, Dave chimed in. "Yeah." He was half-bent as he continued to walk in his feeble attempt to mock an old guy and said, "Look at me. I play golf."

Farmer thought a non-response to Dave's humor was best and said, "Yes, it is for older people, even very old people." He stopped walking and turned his head from side to side, addressing them. "And for young people and middle-aged people too."

It was a coin toss for Dave and Brian: Be heroes when they pinched hit but sit on the bench most of the time; play all the time on Lincoln. They were silent as they thought and walked.

"Tell you what, guys. Talk to your folks about it. Talk to Mr. Henning. Take your time. Let me know what you decide."

Brian said, "Do we play against the girls?"

"No, they're on the girls' team. But you can certainly play with them when the teams aren't playing."

Dave and Brian leaned forward from beneath Farmer's arms and looked at each other. Both raised their eyebrows.

They spoke with their fathers, and both got the same feedback about it being a great game they could play throughout their lives, have a lot of fun, meet many great people, and perhaps become a pro and make tons of money. They spoke with Henning, who objectively answered all their serious and silly questions. The boys decided to join

Lincoln. They were the two youngest team members and the only novices. All that changed when they became high school seniors with a year of golf experience under their belts.

From his parents' point of view, Brian was raised well. He was nourished spiritually, physically, and mentally. From Brian's point of view, he received less attention than he wanted. The only times that he got the attention he sought was with humor. He told jokes and got laughs; he imitated other people and got applause; he played practical jokes on his parents and friends and got their full attention. His sense of humor took on many forms, depending on his mood and the circumstances. Sometimes, he had a dry sense of humor, sometimes dark, sometimes slapstick. Anything that would make people laugh was up his alley. As he matured, he noticed that the recipients of his jokes and joking felt better when they laughed. They seemed happier. He liked that. It jibed with his essential altruistic character. He learned, however, that there was a time and place for humor. His behavior on the high school golf team was one of those lessons.

Among his shenanigans was installing a spring-loaded device in a golf cup. When a golf ball was putted into the hole, the spring sprung, shooting the ball into the air. Team members laughed; Coach Henning did not and chastised him. He super glued golf balls together on the practice range. Again, laughter. Again, chastised. When Henning demonstrated how to swing a wedge for a flop shot, Brian pressed his clicker to distract him, and it worked. Ditto on the reactions. The last straw was the exploding golf ball. When the puff of smoke cleared, Henning told Brian, "Well, Mr. Saddlemeyer, it looks like you prefer to hit a baseball to a golf ball."

Henning was convinced that Dave was complicit in his friend's antics, but without proof, he decided to give him a pass, a pass that was not accepted. Dave offered his resignation from the team. "I don't want to be on the team if Brian's not on it," said Dave. Brian and Dave became team-less for the remainder of his senior year.

***

Dave and Brian laughed almost uncontrollably as they recounted all the silly, weird, and wonderful things they did on the Lincoln golf team. "We had a helluva lot of fun back then," said Dave.

Brian stopped laughing and said, "Yeah, but we were kids. That's all in the past."

"Yeah, in the past. Everything that has happened in our lives is now in the past. And every day we live, we create a new past."

Brian looked somber. "You're getting heavy, Dave."

Dave saw an opening and needed to stay on point. "Yeah, maybe. It strikes me that as we travel through life, we do good and bad things, laugh and cry, cherish the wonders we encounter, and dread the disasters."

Brian looked at him and grimaced. "I know exactly what you're saying, Mr. Philosopher, and where you're going, but let's just shift gears for now. Okay?"

Dave felt he got through to Brian and hoped he remembered the good, the laughs, and the wonders. He didn't want to shift out of a high-speed gear but felt that Brian would park his thoughts if he didn't. Down-shifting, Dave said, "Hey, if not for the golf team, we probably wouldn't be here today, where I am playing much better golf than you are."

Seemingly relaxed, Brian said, "The coach wasn't going to kick you off. So why did you quit?"

Dave nudged Brian's shoulder with his shoulder and said, "I guess I thought it wouldn't be as much fun once you left. It was what it was. Can't change yesterday."

"Shit, Dave. Back to heavy?"

"Okay, I'll shut up. But let me ask you. What would you have done if I was the one that got kicked off?"

"I would have told the coach he was right to kick you off. You had no respect for the game or your fellow teammates."

"You're so full of shit."

Stone-faced, Brian said, "Like you said, you can't change yesterday. I had my chance to incriminate you, and I blew it." He let out a raucous *"Ha!"*

The conversation was muddled with mixed statements, jumping around from serious to silly. Dave decided there was enough serious talk for the time being. *Let it sink in,* he thought.

Brian started to hum a song. "That sounds familiar," said Dave.

"Yesterday made me think of 'Yesterday.' Beatles," said Brian.

Dave was pleased that Brian was humming…singing. *Happy people sing,* he thought. "Great song. Melancholic."

"Appropriate is the best way to describe it."

Not remembering all the lyrics, Dave thought of pursuing what Brian meant. "How's that?"

"All my troubles seemed so far away," said Brian. "Yeah, far away."

Perplexed, Dave asked, "They were, and you overcame them."

Brian stomped on the floor of the golf car and said, "Dammit!"

Dave tried to decipher Brian's words and actions but couldn't. "Dammit?"

He smacked his ankle and said, "Damn ants!"

Dave was in a quandary. He needed to keep Brian talking, hoping it would lead to a revelation, an acceptance of his situation, or it could lead to anger, which might have an emotionally deleterious outcome. "Yeah, lots of ants around these here parts. Sorry, I don't have any ant spray."

Looking straight out, ignoring Dave, Brian recited another lyric. "I'm not half the man I used to be."

Dave thought Brian was making a statement. "You're losing me. Half the man?"

Brian turned to Dave and said, "It's one of the lines in the song. Here's another: 'Why she had to go, I don't know.'"

Dave understood the gravity of Brian's words. He wanted to reach over and hug his friend. He hoped Brian would cry and let it out. "Sorry, Bri. I didn't understand what you were saying. How about we hum a different tune?"

Brian took a long breath. "No sorries, Dave." I agree that it's a nice song. It just cut into me, ya know?

"Yes. 'nough said. Next hole?"

"Sure. I got ants in my pants to play some more."

Dave smiled. "Onward!"

Chapter 10:

Life to Live For

Brian asked Dave to stop as they approached the tee box of the fifth hole.

"Right here, Bri?" Dave asked to confirm.

Brian nodded. "Here's good. I'm going over to that oak tree."

"It's an elm," Dave stated the obvious.

Deviating from his usual behavior since his arrival, Brian didn't miss the opportunity to point it out. "Thank you, Mr. Arborist. I always want to make sure I irrigate the right species."

Dave laughed. "Go for it," he gestured.

"Take your time. No one behind us. I hope everything comes out all right." He gave Brian a big clown-like grin. But that faded soon when Brian didn't laugh or hurl a witticism back at him. He was disappointed but didn't express it, so he just walked off toward the tree.

Walking away, Dave took the opportunity to call Nicole but waited while he viewed a couple of birds in a tree. They were on the same branch, about one foot apart, facing each other. One bird flapped its wings. Then the other. He saw them opening and closing their beaks. He smiled, thinking that they were talking to each other. He decided to have some nonsense fun and do voiceovers. Dave was quirky in that way, or perhaps it would be more accurate to describe him as someone who always found a way to entertain himself.

Imitating a male voice, he said, "Hey, how's it going?"

Imitating a female voice, he replied, "Not well. Building this nest is going slowly. I'm with eggs." Dave snorted with his play on words.

"Bummer. Can I help?" he said, imitating a male voice.

"Twigs. Can you get me some twigs, like in a hurry?"

"Can do."

Curiously, just as Dave said 'can do,' one of the birds flew away. Dave's eyebrows shot up in surprise. *What a coincidence. Maybe they were listening."*

He then said to himself, "You're sick, Mr. Arborist," remembering what Brian had called him in their last interaction a few minutes ago. Remembering what he had intended to do before the birds distracted him, he dialed Nicole but didn't hit the call button. Thinking about his nonsense bird talk, it struck him that it represented his relationship with Brian and his want to help him.

Chuckling at the thought, he finally called Nicole. After the hellos, she said, "I'm in the middle of something. Can I call you back?"

"Sure, love."

"Anything pressing that you have to tell me right now?"

Dave looked up at the bird hovering around her nest. "I just had an allegorical creation that reinforced my wanting to help Brian."

"Really? That's great. I have no idea what the heck you mean."

"Like *Animal Farm.* You know, Snowball and the other animals, but this time it was birds."

Nicole held the phone in front of her scrunched face. Intrigued by Dave's words, she wanted to know what he meant but couldn't pursue the conversation at that moment. "Later. Bye."

Dave looked out at the golf course but didn't see Brian. It seemed he was gone for five minutes or more, which concerned him. He called out but didn't get a response. He walked to the elm and didn't see him. He called out again, louder. Still no response. He phoned Brian, but when he got the recorded hello without the phone ringing, he knew Brian's phone was turned off. He decided riding the golf car could cover more ground faster. His effort was futile. No Brian was to be seen.

"This is Melissa at the pro shop. How can I help you?"

"This is Dave Sherman. I'm at the fifth hole and can't find my partner."

"Did you check the restrooms? The closest ones are at the third and seventh holes. Maybe he's there."

Dave became angry at what he perceived to be a pedantic response. He would have preferred., *Oh my. How can I help?* That's what a customer service person should say. That's what friends say. He contained his anger and calmly and slowly said, "He's been having some problems, like, ah, forgetting things."

"Alzheimer's?"

Dave thought it best to go along with Melissa's diagnosis rather than discuss what kind of problems Brian had. "Yes, I think so. Can you send a ranger out to help me find him?"

She asked for Brian's description and told Dave that a ranger should be arriving within minutes.

***

Brian stood behind the elm, looking right and left to see if anyone could see him. He unzipped and heard a raven croak. The raven looked down at him, continuing with its croaking. Brian looked up and said, "What? You don't want me to piss on your tree?"

The raven responded with a loud croak as if it understood, causing Brian to laugh at the situation.

He looked left and right again and was confident that no one could see him except, perhaps, the golfers on the tee box, one of whom was a woman. He hesitated a little; his chivalrous character suggested he refrain from peeing till the golfers were further away but his

111

bladder disagreed. At the moment, he could only look for a better hide nearby to do his business. He looked around and saw a bigger tree twenty feet away. "I can hold it. Hang in there, pecker," Brian grunted as he zipped his pants back up, clearly having a difficult time holding his bladder for too long.

Laughing at himself for his pecker pun, he walked to the bigger tree, spied the surroundings, and was about to unzip when he heard, "Hey there. Need to pee?"

When he turned around, he saw a portly man with a shock of wavy white hair signaling him. "Well, yeah."

"I have a john in my casita. My wife hated it when guys pissed on the trees. Come on in."

Brian accepted the invitation, peed, and thanked the guy. "I'm Frank," said the guy. "Want a beer?"

Brian looked at the guy up and down. He thought *Frank* was a coincidentally appropriate name. *Is he just lonely?* came to mind, and then *serial killer?* He wondered why negative thoughts popped up first. *Just a nice guy* was his next thought." Sure. That would be great, but my friend is waiting for me."

"Okay. How's a beer to go?"

Brian instinctively wanted to say, "I just went," but he decided to be polite. "Great. Thanks."

Frank retrieved a couple of beers from his casita, handed one to Brian, and, looking a tad sullen, said, "Well, then, just a toast if you don't mind. Here's to my wife. May she rest in peace and thank me for not letting you piss on a tree." He held up his bottle, waiting for Brian to reciprocate.

"Rest in peace, Frank?"

He explained that his wife passed away almost a year ago. "Heart." He looked down and remained silent for a few seconds. He looked up to the skies and said, "Miss you." He fought off the feeling of tears welling up. "Sorry. By the way, I didn't get your name."

"Brian. Brian Saddlemeyer. I lost my wife six months ago, almost to the day."

"Heart?"

"Cancer."

"Join me for a minute," said Frank.

Brian clinked his bottle of beer with Frank's. "Nice words, Frank." They took a sip and stood still, eyes looking at eyes, each projecting their sad thoughts.

"Have a seat, my friend," said Frank. "I'm sure your friend will understand that you needed to take a very long piss." Both of them laughed.

"Yeah," said Frank. "I'm a retired pastor, and I could turn to God to help me. But what keeps me going are my gal's last words just before she went into surgery: 'Don't give up. There's a lot of life to live for.' It was like she knew she wouldn't survive the surgery."

Brian felt a shiver run down his body. It was visible to Frank. "You okay, Brian?"

"Yeah. Just got a chill from the cold beer."

Frank didn't buy Brian's cold beer chill. He had gone through the same kind of reactions for months following his wife's passing whenever he spoke about her. "I'm here if you want to talk about it."

Brian composed himself. He placed his beer on the table and shook Frank's hand. "Thank you again. My partner's waiting."

Frank knew he would not see Brian again. He knew Brian was struggling with his wife's death. He knew this was the only chance to give Brian food for thought about life and death. "Are you a religious man, Brian Saddlemeyer?"

Shiver gone, Brian sat erect in an almost guarded posture. "No, not really. I believe in God, but I don't practice a religion. I don't go to church if that is what you mean."

Frank leaned forward on his chair. He wanted to be closer to Brian and connect with him emotionally. "I'm not an evangelist," he said. "I believe you lay out the facts and let a person decide what to do with their life."

"What facts?"

Frank spoke on about his past life and, without chest-beating, told Brian about all the good he had done in his life. He gave several examples of how his involvement helped someone to be a better person or deal with a loss. "You strike me as a good guy, so I bet you did lots of good things to help people."

Brian couldn't deny his words. If asked to do so, he could have rattled off dozens of situations where he had helped people. *So what?* Brian thought, but he said, "Yeah, I feel good about some of the things I've done, but that was in the past. It's over."

"Is it, Brian?"

Brian's frozen stare at his beer bottle told Frank his words might have impacted him. Feeling that Brian might be open to delving further into his grief and questioning life, Frank continued with his words of apparent wisdom. "Other than in your heart and in your memories, where is your wife now?"

Brian knew Frank wanted him to say heaven. He was, after all, a pastor. But Frank decided to be honest with his feelings. "Her body is six feet under, decaying. When I visit her grave, I try hard not to see her there and …" His voice quivered, his hand became limp, and his beer fell and smashed on the travertine patio tiles.

"I'm sorry, Frank. It slipped. Let me clean it up."

Frank rose from his chair and put his hands on Brian's shoulders. "You're carrying a very heavy burden on your shoulders. It's affecting your heart and your mind. You think of only the past, your loss. To paraphrase my wife's words, live for the life that lies ahead."

The spilled beer was evaporating in the heat of the day. The shards of brown beer bottle glass reflected the sun and looked more like art than garbage. Brian bowed his head and closed his eyes. Tears welled. His body shook as he cried. Frank held his shoulders, increasing his grip to tell Brian his life matters, that it isn't over.

Frank offered Brian a paper towel to dry his eyes. As Brian did so, he added more icing to his encouraging words. "I read a book by a guy named Albert Pike. When I gave the eulogy for a close friend who died some years back, I quoted Pike. 'What we have done for ourselves alone dies with us; what we have done for others and the world remains and is immortal.' I think you're like my friend."

Brian was drained. He heard similar words from Dave, as well as quotes and metaphors about golf and life. His head spun, his mouth agape. He put his hands on Frank's hands. His eyes thanked him for his compassion.

"Are you Brian?" asked the ranger who had pulled his golf car up to the fence in the back of Frank's house.

"Yeah, that's me."

"Mr. Sherman is looking for you."

Brian pursed his lips, nodded several times to Frank, shook his hand with both hands, and departed.

***

Brian got out of the ranger's golf car and into Dave's. "Sorry, Dave."

"You must have one heck of a big bladder. What happened? Where'd you go?"

Brian recounted his journey from the elm to the oak to the casita. Dave asked, "You talked to a bird? So did I. Well, not *to* a bird. I talked *as* a bird."

Brian's raised eyebrows showed his surprise at what Dave said. Half a second later, his squirrelly face showed his confusion. "*As a bird? Like tweet, tweet?*"

"Forget it. So what's with that guy?"

"His wife died a year ago."

"You're bullshittin' me." His body slumped, and he said, "No, I didn't mean that. I mean, well…I don't know what I mean."

Brian said, "Coincidence. I think the word you're looking for is coincidence."

"Yeah, double coincidence. Birds and, well, wives."

Brian gestured with his finger pointed forward and said, "Forward. Next tee."

As they drove for the next hundred feet to the tee box, Dave wanted to ask Brian what he and Frank discussed but thought his shut mouth would open Brian's mouth. It didn't.

A foursome in front of them walked onto the tee box, all twenty-something. Both men were holding a beer can. Both women were dressed to the nines and looked more like they were going to a dance club than a golf course. Dave noticed a large cooler strapped to the top of the basket between the driver and the golf bags. He suspected it was full of beer. "What do you think is in the cooler, Bri?"

Sounding serious, Bri said, "A year's supply of Mary Jane. Do they still call it that?

Dave took Brian's comment in the humorous spirit with which it was meant. He disliked that he had to quickly analyze *where* Brian was coming from rather than simply reacting to the words he heard. He needed to walk a fine line before he said anything. "I think it's all hidden in between a few six-packs. And, yes, Mary Jane, or weed, pot, grass, ganja…the list goes on."

"Let 'em go. Let 'em have fun. We're in no hurry," said Brian.

Dave smiled inwardly, liking Brian's open-minded, nonjudgmental take on the foursome. It was the polar opposite of his reaction to the twosome that lost a golf club.

Pleased with what he thought was Brian's intent to take a break, Dave agreed with him. He pulled his golf car to the dirt and gravel area under a shady tree. They sat there, not saying a word for a minute or so. Dave tried to clear his mind by focusing on the beauty of the golf course, the geese feeding on the grass, and the cloudless sky. Brian couldn't let go of Frank's words, words that reinforced what Dave was telling him, words that were battling his grief. He slowly and rhythmically strummed his fingers on the dashboard as his mind tried to pull itself into reality. Dave guessed Brian was thinking about his life and not, thank goodness, playing a tune in his head. Anxious to know Brian's thoughts, he broke the silence. "So, you want to talk about your chat with Frank?"

"Not really. Not now. I just want to chew on what he said."

"I hope he said good things."

"Yes, good things."

Chapter 11:

A Wrong Turn, a Good Turn

A series of loud screams jolted Dave and Brian.

"What the hell?" said Dave, shaken by the sudden noise.

Brian was contemplating Frank's words and Dave's emotion-kicking, memory-reminding tactics. Both men profoundly affected Brian's emotions, specifically the plan he had in mind following his visit with Dave. Hearing what Dave said, he turned the dial on his thoughts and responded. "What?"

"The screaming. Don't you hear it?" Dave asked him, wondering why Brian couldn't hear it.

"Yeah. Maybe one of them got a hole-in-one." Brian shrugged, followed by a dry chuckle.

Dave, clearly not satisfied with the answer, cupped his ear to listen more carefully. "It's not a happy scream. Something's wrong."

With a snort, Brian said, "Probably that chick in the very short skirt realizing she forgot to put underwear on."

Dave appreciated the joke, but when the screaming continued, he knew whatever caused it was not a joke. "Maybe she saw a coyote," said Dave. "They tend to roam on golf courses, rabbit hunting."

Brian wanted to get back to contemplating. "I'm tellin' you, Dave, it was the panties."

In the distance, they saw a man and woman jumping up and down next to their golf car. Dave and Brian didn't see the other golf car. Dave grabbed his range finder to see what he could see. "One of the golf cars is in the lake," he said. "I only see the top of it."

Dave raced his golf car toward the foursome. When he arrived, he saw a face-down woman in the shallow end, her sprawled legs in the water. Her outstretched mud-covered arms suggested she tried to break her fall when she was hurled from the car. A man was lying on his back on the muddy shore, bleeding from his head. Dave and Brian saw the other man, apparently traumatized, sitting in his golf car, mouth open, gazing at the situation. The other woman was still screaming, hopping around without knowing what to do.

Brian jumped out of the golf car and onto the mud at the crash site. The one-hour triage class he took during his first year in dental school paid off. "Dave, call the pro shop and get an ambulance out here. Now!"

"Not 911?" Dave asked in confusion.

Brian yelled, "Pro Shop! Now!" Dave, without any further question, ran to comply.

Brian checked the man's pulse and found it beating. He checked the woman's pulse. It was also beating. Doing a superficial check of the bodies, he couldn't find any injury save the gash on the man's head. With both breathing and not knowing if there were any broken bones, he let them stay in their current positions.

He yelled to the guy, "Throw me a towel." The guy didn't move. He yelled at the woman to get a towel, but her panicky state continued.

Dave went to his golf bag to untie his towel, but Brian didn't wait. He pulled off his golf shirt, compressed it into a ball, placed it on the man's wound, and applied pressure.

Waiting for an ambulance to arrive, he kept an eye on the woman lying in the mud. She was still unconscious but thankfully still breathing. He looked across to the other side of the lake and saw four people standing at the lake's edge. "Geez! I don't believe it," he said as he saw two of them pointing their cell phones at the accident site. He yelled, hoping they could hear him from one hundred yards away, "No, these folks don't need your help, assholes. They're just resting after a grueling round."

Dave reported that the pro shop is contacting 911, and they're sending a ranger out who's trained in emergency care. "Great, Dave. After you slap that girl and make her stop screaming, clear the area of the two cars so an ambulance can pull up close,"

Dave commanded the survivors to follow him as he drove their car a reasonable distance from the accident site. A couple of rangers pulled up. One was an EMT. He took over from Brian next to the bleeding guy. The other ranger went to the still traumatized lady.

In a record-breaking five minutes, the fire department medical unit arrived. All was well in hand. Dave and Brian thanked the rangers and fire department folks and drove back to the dirt and gravel area under the shady tree.

"I'm calling the pro shop again, Bri. You need a change of clothing."

"My pants will be dry in five minutes, and I like muddy shoes."

"Shirt."

"I think the med guys are going to use it for gauze. I kind of like the bare-chested look."

"Club rules. You have to wear a collared shirt."

"Okay, fine. But only because I don't want to make other guys jealous when they see my manly pecs."

Dave refrained from saying *Everything's a joke to you. Is your humor keeping you in denial about life?* He asked the pro shop to bring a large, plain white golf shirt to the tee box at the fifth hole. "Hurry, please." Wanting to connect with Brian, and added, "People are staring at Dr. Saddlemeyer's manly torso."

"Don't hang up, Dave!" said Brian. "I don't want a large white shirt."

"Black? Blue? Yellow?"

Brian said, "White's okay, but make it a medium to fit better on my few pounds times ten.

Hearing Brian joke about his appearance was a far cry from how he responded to Dave at Sky Harbor. He thought the change might have been his conversation with Frank or all of the conversations he and Brian had. *Was it the lake accident?* he thought. *Did his automatic reactions remind him of who he is?*

"You were impressive, my friend. The way you took over at the lake was fantastic."

"Yeah, thanks. But anyone could have done what I did."

"Hate to disagree, but you're wrong. The guy with the drunken gaze and the screaming idiot couldn't do what you did. You did a very good thing."

A very good thing buzzed in his head. That's what Frank said. Hearing it again resonated. "Yeah, but I needed your help, so thanks for helping. We did it together."

"Fine. Together. But you get top billing."

Brian fanned his hand and turned away.

"Bri, you're the most unselfish and generous guy I've ever known. I only heard about a few people that you helped. Tom told me. But I bet there were dozens."

"Okay. Fine. I helped a few people occasionally, but it's no biggie."

Dave stepped out of the golf car, put his hands on the roof, and leaned over to talk to Brian. "Well, let's start with Erickson."

"Okay. I helped him. I was just returning the favor."

"Right. Returning a favor. And that gal Allison who worked at your reception desk. Did you return a favor?"

"I hated losing her, but I lent her some money when she told me her passion was to be a professional pianist and couldn't afford music school. Big deal."

Dave nodded a few times. "Yeah, it was a big deal. Don't you see that?"

"She paid me back."

"That's not the point. How about that landscape maintenance guy you had who now has a major commercial landscaping company?"

"That was Charlotte's doing. She made fliers for him."

"Where did he get the money to buy a new truck and tools, and who knows what?"

"Enough, Dave."

"How many young dentists did you tutor, free of charge? How many financially struggling people smile when they hear your name?"

"Hey, you've helped a lot of people too."

"And you know, Bri, I won't stop helping. You shouldn't either."

The power line buzzing sound of a grackle looking down at them from a tree limb was the only sound they could hear as they sat without speaking.

"Hi, guys." Melissa from the pro shop arrived and gave Brian a white golf shirt and a gift card. "The shirt's on the house," she said.

"What's the card for?" he asked.

"Aaron, our EMT guy, told us what you did. We appreciate that and want to show our appreciation."

"Sure, thanks." He handed the card to Dave. "Here, Dave, you have it. I won't be needing anything from the pro shop."

Dave was disturbed, back to feeling the yo-yo effect brought on by Brian's manic-depressive behavior.

"Here we go again, Bri?" asked Dave.

"Here we go again, what?" Brian gave him a puzzled look.

Dave sighed and said, "You gave me the gift card because you won't need it. What the hell does that mean?"

Brian did not have a slip of the tongue. He knew he would never visit that pro shop again and genuinely believed he didn't need any golf stuff. He felt better and more optimistic about life but wasn't ready to tell Dave his thoughts. "I have every conceivable thing there is to have to play golf. Clubs, tees, shoes, socks, shirts, jackets, hats. Hell, everything. I'm donating all of it to Goodwill, so why the hell should I buy something new and then carry it there?"

"Goodwill? Everything?"

"As I told you, Dave, I'm not enjoying golf as much as I used to. This is my last round. Oh, I see where you're going. You want some of my golf stuff, don't you?

"Stay put, guys," said the ranger who pulled up beside their golf car. "Have to close this hole."

Brian looked at the ranger's name badge and said, "Glad you're here, Eric. Dave here wants all of my golf equipment and is holding me hostage till I give it to him. Do you have a gun?"

Dave's eyes shot up. The ranger played along and pretended to make a call on his walkie-talkie. "Base, Eric, on five tee-box. Hostage situation. Send armed cops."

The three men smiled at the silliness of the situation. Dave asked, "Closing it because of the accident?"

"Yup. Won't be long, but you might want to skip this hole and come back to it later."

"We're not in any rush. Okay, if we just sit and wait?" asked Dave.

Eric called Base, this time for real, and asked for a timing estimate. Dave heard the response and decided to skip the hole. He told Brian, "About a half-hour wait. Let's go to the next hole, okay?"

"I like this spot. Let's wait here, okay?" said Brian.

Dave hoped Brian wanted to talk about his thoughts about life…his struggles with life. "Sure."

Eric drove to the car path next to the tee box to inform approaching golfers that the hole was closed for a while. When they were out of earshot of Eric, Dave asked, "What's on your mind, my friend?"

Brian inhaled slowly and exhaled sharply. He looked out at the idyllic vista that surrounded him. It was peacefully quiet except for the water splashing on rocks in the nearby brook and birds chirping--sounds that added to the peaceful aesthetic of the place. He saw a goose leading six goslings across a grassy knoll and smiled at himself when he thought *That goose has all its goslings in a row. So did the ducks, and so do I, I think.* He wanted to tell Dave about his plan -- why he agreed to come to Arizona and play one last round of golf with him, but decided to chat a bit about Frank, which cascaded to telling Dave Frank's observation about life.

The conversation ceased and the vista vanished when he heard a nearby loud "Fore!" causing him to nearly jump out of his seat.

Chapter 12:

A Turn in the Events

A golf car pulled up next to Dave. "Is that you, Dave?" said the driver.

"Oh man, what year is this?" Brian groaned in a low voice, but Dave heard him clearly.

Chuckling, Dave said, "That's Lenny. He always wears that vintage stuff. I guess he thinks people will look at his outfit and not see his lousy golf shots."

"Lenny!" said Dave. "Good to see you."

Dressed in checkered golf knickers, argyle socks, a shirt emblazoned with the American flag, and a Kelly green tam o' shanter, Lenny stroked his hand in front of his outfit and said, "Whaddaya think?"

Taking a step back and tilting his head up and down, Dave said, "They're the nicest three outfits I've ever seen." He ended with a nod of approval.

Brian raised his hand in greeting. "Hi. I'm Dave's best friend. Have been for years. I'm trying to sell him my golf clubs, but he's a cheap SOB."

Lenny gave him a quizzical look and was about to say something when he was interrupted by a thunderous roar in the sky. Brian turned white with fear and ducked, "What the hell?"

Dave, Lenny, and Lenny's partner, Bill, laughed. "Hey, Chicken Little, it's the sound of freedom," said Lenny. "Isn't it great?"

Brian stood up. "The sound of freedom? What the hell is that?"

Roar again. Brian ducked again, prompting another round of laughter from Dave, Lenny, and Bill. Lenny said, "They're F-16s out of Luke. Practicing. Don't usually fly around here, but I guess they can go anywhere they want."

Brian relaxed. "If they fly over during my downswing, am I allowed a mulligan?"

For a third time, the three guys laughed, joined in by Brian, who made a chicken-wing gesture with bent arms.

Lenny explained that he had to intervene in an employee dispute at his factory. "I thought *retired* would at least let me play a round of uninterrupted golf. I should have sold the business and got on with life."

Brian excused himself from the group to ostensibly pee behind a tree. He walked to the brook and partially placed his shoe in the water, moving it slowly left and right, watching the mud dissolve in the sloshing water. He repeated the move with his other foot, all the time watching the goose and its gaggle. His shoes were cleaned, and to some extent, his mind was cleansed of disturbing thoughts. *Sound of freedom,* he thought. *Has a nice ring to it.*

Dave told Lenny, "You know there's a wait on this hole, don't you?"

"Yeah, but I can't wait. Can't even play the next hole, dammit."

Dave nodded. "Yup, things interrupt life."

"It's not so bad," said Lenny, "Besides, I don't much care for this new course. I find it too difficult for my level of play."

Dave nodded as a courtesy and complimented Lenny to feed his ego. "I've seen you hit some fantastic shots when we've played. I think this course is just not used to your level of play and is purposely working against you."

Lenny's ego appreciated the compliment, but his humility surfaced. "You have a way of bullshitting that I don't find offensive." Both guys smiled.

"We might call it a day after nine holes," said Dave.

"If you do, drop in on 'The Turn' near the ninth green. It's like a restaurant and lounge, not just a piss stop." Lenny looked at his watch and pointed his finger at it, saying, without words, "I have to go."

"Business before pleasure," said Dave. "I understand. See ya."

"And you won't believe this, but all the paintings on the walls are of nudes. See ya."

Dave said, "Yup. Onward, bud. Let's connect and try this course again."

"Yup. See ya."

Dave nodded and said, "Nude paintings?"

Lenny drove off, smiling, without answering Dave's question. Five seconds later, he made a U-turn. "I forgot to ask you. How's Nicole doing?"

Dave realized Lenny's question was not like *Hey, how ya doin'?* The look on Lenny's face was one of compassion. The tone of his voice suggested he was concerned. Dave paused. The timing was not good. He anticipated a heart-to-heart talk with Brian while they sat in the shade. As much as he wanted to know what Lenny meant, his priority for the moment was Brian. "Fine. Just fine."

Lenny went on. "Yeah, I know stuff like that could be upsetting. My wife Shelly went through it. Turned out fine, so I'm sure Nicole will be fine. I'm glad Nicole told her about it, and I'm sure she gave Nicole some comforting words."

Dave was speechless. Lenny looked at his watch again and said, "Shit. Gotta go. Hit 'em straight and far." He and his partner drove off. Dave stood still, looking in Lenny's direction, but could not see anything. Disturbing thoughts clouded his vision.

When he saw Lenny drive off, Brian returned to Dave's golf car to see Dave holding tight on the steering wheel and pushing forward and backward. His anger was unmistakable. "Lenny piss you off, Dave? What did he say?" asked Brian.

Dave didn't respond.

"Dave. What's up? You okay?"

Dave took his phone from the dashboard and dialed Nicole as he walked away, keeping Brian in the dark as to why.

Nicole's phone rang three times. Dave felt it was five minutes between rings. *Answer the damn phone, Nicole. Answer it!*

"Hi, Dave. I was about to call you about your bird thing. And Brian, of course."

Dave took a breath to calm himself. He didn't want to sound angry even though anger built in him when he realized Nicole had a problem – probably a medical problem – and didn't share it with him. As calmly as he could, he said, "Nicole. I just found out that you have a medical problem. At least, I think it's medical. You didn't tell me about it. What is it?"

"Hold on, Dave." Nicole pressed her phone to her chest to mute the sound and told Missy that she needed to have a private chat with Dave. "I'm back, Dave. Do you really want to talk about this now? Aren't you with Brian?"

"Screw Brian. No, I don't mean that. Yeah, I'm with Brian and having a hell of a time dealing with him. But what we need to talk about right now is far more important."

"I know you're upset with me for keeping a secret, but I wasn't going to keep it forever. I just put it in the cupboard and planned on telling you after Brian left. I mean, after you resolved the issues with him."

Brian noticed Dave's panic-like movements as he walked around, phone to ear. "Everything okay, Dave?"

"Hold on, Nicole." Dave put his phone against his chest and told Brian that he needed to talk to Nicole about a problem that had just come up. His eyes flashed, but Brian rejected the signal.

"Just came up?" asked Brian. "You called her, so the problem seems to be something about Lenny." Brian put his hand on Dave's shoulder. "Please don't tell me that you suspect Lenny and Nicole are having an affair."

Dave bellowed, "Christ's sake, Bri! No! No affair. Something else. I'll tell you later."

Brian was shocked by Dave's outburst. He gave him a tight-lipped smile, nodded, and returned to the golf car.

Dave didn't take another breath to calm himself and blurted out, "What the hell happened? What didn't you tell me?"

Nicole asked Dave if they could have the conversation after golf was finished and he was at home. "No," replied Dave. "Now. Please."

Nicole didn't immediately respond. She thought about lying. She thought about skirting the issue. She didn't know how to tell him but knew she had to. "I had a mammogram. They found what could be a cancerous nodule."

"Cancer?"

"Yes, cancer. Well, maybe cancer. I don't know yet."

Dave was more upset hearing the word cancer than he was by Nicole keeping it a secret. "My golf game just ended. I should be in Flagstaff in about five hours."

"No, Dave, don't come. It's totally unnecessary."

Dave didn't buy the *unnecessary*. He was beside himself, hearing her words. "You have cancer, and you don't think it's necessary for me to be with you?"

Nicole took a breath. She wanted to calm Dave and knew that giving him the top line of the situation was insufficient. "When the nurse, the tech, looked at the mammogram, she said, *Hmm.*"

"What the hell does 'hmm' mean?" he asked.

"Hush. Let me finish. I asked her what that meant, but she skirted the issue and told me the radiologist would get back to me in a few days."

Dave kicked what he thought was a pine cone but discovered it was a slightly erupted tree root. "Owe! Shit!" he said.

"Owe?" said Nicole.

"Never mind. Then what happened?"

"Let me back up. I thought about the 'hmm.' Did some research. The mammogram might have detected a fibroadenoma, a cyst, PASH, or nothing. That's why I'm in Flagstaff."

"I don't have any idea what all those things are. But I do know what cancer is. I don't get it. What the hell does Flagstaff have to do with it? Are you saying you needed to be with our daughter because you might have cancer and wanted to tell her face-to-face but didn't want to tell me?"

Nicole felt the anger in Dave's tone. She knew that the anger he expressed outward overshadowed the compassion he felt inside. "Dave, please do me a favor. Let's continue this discussion in five minutes."

"Why wait?"

"So you can calm down and allow me to explain the whole situation—honest, love. I know you love me, and you know I love you. But we're hitting speed bumps while we're having this talk. We need to get on a smother road. Five minutes? Okay?"

"Four."

"I'll call you in four minutes." Nicole hung up. Dave looked at his phone and made sure it was sufficiently charged. He also noted the time.

When he returned to the golf car, Brian asked what was happening again. Matter-of-factly, Dave told him that Nicole's mammogram indicated she might have cancer. "She's in Flagstaff, and I don't know why she's there. She's going to call me back in four minutes." Dave looked at the time on his phone. "Three and half minutes."

Anxiety causes seconds to feel like minutes and minutes to feel like hours. Dave paced around the golf car. He thought of driving to the clubhouse, ending his round of golf, and high-tailing it up to Flagstaff regardless of what Nicole would tell him when she called back.

Brian was beside himself with indecision: console Dave or stay out of his way. He thought it was interesting that Dave had gone to great lengths to be with him, and probably for the sole purpose of helping him get a grip on his grief. Now, thought Brian, not only did he have a different focus, but he probably also needed help dealing with the situation. Brian uttered a soft grunt to relieve stress. Dave's phone rang at the same time.

"It's me," said Dave.

"Are we on a smoother road? No bumps?"

Dave had calmed down. He knew Nicole wanted to take a break so he could discuss her situation calmly. This was not the first time he and Nicole had a blow-up, but every time they did, it was resolved because both agreed to stay calm and discuss their differences. "I'm on a smooth road and all ears."

"The mammogram was two days before Brian was to arrive. The radiologist's report was due tomorrow."

Dave was calm enough to realize why Nicole kept her mammogram a secret. "You didn't want me to tell Brian to cancel, did you?"

"No, love. You would have been faced with a dilemma. That's when I decided to go to Flagstaff. Richard's good friend is an oncologist, and his good friend is a radiologist. Our wonderful son-in-law arranged for me to see him, have a biopsy, and get the results very soon."

"What's *very soon?*"

"This afternoon. I'll know just about the same time you finish playing golf, and with hope, the same time you tell me that everything went okay with Brian."

"I can't play anymore. You know that."

"You need to."

"No, love. I need to be with you, not with Brian."

"Hold on a moment."

Nicole had another secret that she chose not to divulge. Brian's son asked Nicole not to tell Dave or his dad that he would surprise them with a visit. She believed that Tom's visit would be helpful to Dave in dealing with Brian and helpful to Brian by having his son at his side. She needed a moment to conjure a convincing reason for Dave to stay put without lying to him.

***

Tom Saddlemeyer was a dedicated surgeon, husband, father, and, given his actions for the last six months, a very dedicated son, too. His intervention at his father's suicide attempt three months ago saved his father's life and reinforced his love for him. Tom's weekly calls to his dad and the several visits he made to see his father in Seattle convinced Tom that his father was effectively dealing with the loss of his wife.

Brian lived in two personality states. Following his suicide attempt, he thought the best way to not drag Tom into his grief and to protect him was to be a brave and sane person who wanted to continue to live. It was the antithesis of the man Dave witnessed.

Tom was to attend a medical convention in Scottsdale, at which he was to speak about his experiences and findings while performing bypass surgeries. It was a one-day in-and-out commitment that didn't allow any time to drop in on Dave Sherman to say hello. As he disembarked from his flight to Phoenix, he received a call from the organizer asking if he could delay his speech to the next day due to various changes in the speakers' agendas. Tom agreed and thought he would surprise Dave and Nicole with a visit, and possibly spend the night at their home.

He called Dave, who saw it was Tom calling, and decided the timing was not right for a chat with Brian's son. When Dave's voicemail message came on, he disconnected and called Nicole. He happily discovered that Dave was not only in town, but his dad was with him at Palms. He asked Nicole not to let Dave or his dad know. "I have a photo on my phone that will be very appropriate to show them today."

He called Palms.

"This is Melissa at Palms Golf Club. How can I help you?"

"Hi. This is Tom Saddlemeyer. I believe Dave Sherman is playing there today."

Melissa told him to hold on while she checked her computer. "Yes. They're a twosome."

"Where do you think they are now?"

Melissa found the question odd since she told him they were playing golf at the Palms.

"What do you mean?"

Tom was a tolerant and forgiving person, a trait taught to him by his father. He didn't question Melissa's intellect and said, "About which hole?"

Melissa informed him when they teed off and said they should be finished at about two o'clock. "So they'll be at the turn about noon, would you say?"

Melissa agreed.

***

133

Despite their fundamental character differences, Dave and Nicole were on the same wavelength on almost all issues throughout their marriage. When disagreements surfaced, they were amicably resolved. When decisions needed to be made, they were made in total agreement. Dave was always the planner, the chess player thinking about the next ten moves. Nicole was a Tic-Tak-Toe person, reacting to the next move. Dave's nickname for Nicole was Que Sera Sera, and both would laugh at it. Nicole was living up to her nickname with her thoughts about the biopsy. Her views about it were anathema to Dave.

"I'm back," said Nicole. She convinced Dave to continue playing and helping Brian by reinforcing that by the time he could be in Flagstaff, she would already have the biopsy results. "It would be a wasted trip, Dave."

"Being with you is never a waste. And being with you in case, God forbid, the biopsy is not favorable…well, I'm just having a tug-of-war about all of this. Help Brian, be at your side." He screamed out of frustration.

"Hey, Mr. Planner. Priority number one right now is Brian. You have him in your clutches. Help him. Priority two is me. I can totally handle this situation."

Hearing Dave scream, Brian rushed to his side and insisted that Dave tell him what was happening. After he gave Brian a top-line summary of the situation, Brian said, "She's Nicole. She can totally handle the situation."

Chapter 13:

In Charge

"I can't just sit here. Let's skip five and go to six," said Dave as he stepped into the golf car. His expression reflected a bit of annoyance, probably because he disliked where he parked.

Brian shrugged, "You're in charge, my handsome chauffeur." He wanted to know all the details of Nicole's situation but didn't want to upset him with a bunch of questions. Dave's uncharacteristic outburst when he asked if Nicole and Lenny were having an affair told Brian to keep his mouth shut till Dave opened his. It was not like Brian to be walking on eggshells around Dave; it was the other way around since he had arrived.

"Sixth hole. Par 4," said Brian. "Ya know, I like these tee box signs. The way they show the layout of the hole. This one's a dogleg left. 325 yards. Two-ten to the bunker on the left. Driver, then a mid-iron or maybe a pitch, one putt, birdie." Brian kept voicing his observations, hoping it would help ease the 'situation,' but when he got no response, he turned to look at Dave, who remained in the golf car and looked like he was sleeping with his eyes open.

"You with me, Dave? Dave!" he shouted.

Dave shook when he heard Brian yell his name and blinked a few times before saying, "What?"

"Ready to lose another hole?" Brian challenged, knowing that Dave would never let go of a chance to beat him. But something was off; Dave didn't react as Brian expected.

Dave didn't smile. It wasn't in him. He couldn't disagree with Nicole that he didn't need to be with her, but the pit in his stomach told him he needed to. "Where are we, he asked?"

"Sixth hole. Par 4. I guess you didn't hear me the first time."

"No, sorry."

Brian became energetic and finger-smacked the golf car's plastic canopy like bongo drums. His head moved with the beats, and he sang along, "Rap a tap tap, bam bam boom."

Dave didn't respond in any way. "If I hadn't become a dentist, I think I would have made it big as a drummer in a rock band," Brian said, expecting a sarcastic remark from Dave.

He looked down at Dave. Still no response.

Pursing his lips, Brian thought to try something else. Another tactic crossed his mind, and he said, "So, what's the news?" He frowned when there was no response. He was getting agitated. Raising his voice, he said, "Dave! So what's the news?"

"Dave jolted, looked up at Brian, and said, "Haven't you been listening to a word I said?" He shook his head in disgust.

Consolingly, Brian said, "Dave, baby. You're the one that hasn't been listening. I know you're waiting for Nicole to call you. I know you're very concerned, maybe even scared."

Dave sighed and exited the golf car. Walking a few steps, he looked down at the bark chips scattered around a tree. Turning to Brian, he asked in annoyance, "So why the hell did you ask me if there was any news?"

Brian gave him a sympathetic look and walked to him. Resting his hand on Dave's shoulder, he began in a soft voice, a rare thing to witness of Brian. "Hey, look at me." His tone caught Dave off guard, and he had to comply. "One of the reasons I came here was because you told me you had some news. I was asking about that."

"Look out," said Dave.

Brian said, "Huh?" just as a golf car pulled up close to them.

"You guys playing or resting?" the guy asked, making Brian turn to look at him and back to Dave. Then, he waved his hand, giving them visual permission to play through, and said, "Taking a break."

Brian walked to the golf car, sat inside, reclined as much as he could, and closed his eyes. Dave continued his inspection of the bark chips. Minutes ticked by.

Brian's memory bank opened a window to an incident twenty years ago. Eyes opened, he stepped out of the golf car and went to Dave, sitting on the ground, his back resting against the tree. Another window opened to a bunch of movies he had seen depicting a pensive person leaning on a tree. Gary Cooper, who was playing in "Sergeant York," took hold. *Was he leaning against a bolder on a mountain or a tree?* he questioned.

"It was a boulder, not a tree," he said.

"What was a boulder?" Dave asked curiously, thinking about what Brian was mumbling about. He looked at Brian, his head pointed up, and his eyes closed, and he understood that he was reliving some far-off memory in his mind.

Swinging his golf club across the bark as if he were getting rid of debris, Brian said, "Oh, sorry. I was thinking about something. Yo, bud. You have to keep something in mind. Nicole is an extraordinarily level-headed and competent gal who can handle any situation. Remember the incident at the cabin?" With that, Brian took Dave down memory lane.

***

"You okay back there, Sweety?"

"A-huh."

"This is beautiful, isn't, said Dave."

Nicole continued to scan the scenery. "Sure is. I love the colors. Talk about vibrant. And the serenity." Her eyes were aglow at the wonder.

Dave continued his drive through the thick forest on the narrow dirt road. "We should be at the cabin in less than an hour," he informed.

"I can't wait," said Nicole, excitement evident in her tone. "But I don't want to stop looking at these trees. I wish the sun would stay in the same position the whole time we're here," she added.

"I know somebody who knows somebody that can stop the earth's rotation," said Dave.

Nicole smiled. "Call him. Make sure he knows it's ten in the morning right now." She turned toward the back seat and said, "Missy, my dear. You're missing the scenery."

"I've seen it before," Missy shrugged and flipped a page of the book she was holding, "and I love reading this book."

"Which one are you on?" Dave glanced at the rearview mirror from the corner of his eyes, making sure not to lose his focus on the road.

"'Homeward Bound.' It's a little young for me, but I like the humor, and it's a quick read." Nicole and Dave smiled at each other, cherishing that they had a bright, lovely daughter. "You take after your mother," said Dave.

Without looking up, Missy replied, "I know. Mom also loves to read."

Dave didn't know if Missy was pulling his leg or serious with her reply – he accepted her response with a smile and said, "That and your looks. You certainly inherited her genes."

Missy raised her index finger, hoping Dave would see it in his rearview mirror. "Just a sec." She finished reading the paragraph and said, "I'm glad I didn't inherit your genes, Dad."

He smiled but feigned hurt, and holding a hand to his chest, he said, "Ouch! And why's that?"

Laughing, Missy said, "Then I'd have to shave, and I don't

want to."

Forty minutes later, the scenery changed. They stood in front of their car, looking at the lakeside cabin. The sun was high. The lake shimmered from its rays. The surrounding mountains were a blaze of color. They were mesmerized.

"I can't wait to get on that boat, throw out a line, and just be lazy," said Dave.

"Go take a look. You're off the hook for unloading the car. Missy and I will handle it."

"Ar, ar, ar," said Dave in a deep voice while walking to the rickety dock.

Dave took a giant breath on the dock, stretched his arms out wide, and spoke out. "Look out, fish, I'ma comin'." He stepped down onto the rowboat. It drifted away from the dock. As he fell into the water, he screamed out.

Hearing his scream, Nicole looked out from the cabin and saw a splash. She instantly knew the cry wasn't a *Yahoo, I'm going swimming*. "Missy, get my phone from my purse and run to the dock."

Dave was floating face down, unconscious, and starting to sink. Nicole jumped into the eight feet of water, disregarding the almost freezing cold. Holding the dock with one hand, she turned his body face up. He was too heavy to lift onto the pier, and she was not skilled enough to swim to the shore, holding him above water. "Missy, get the rope over there. Hold one end and throw the other end to me." Nicole wrapped the rope around Dave and told Missy to pull the rope as hard as she could.

Missy struggled to pull the heavy rope. When the slack ended, she cried out. "I can't pull anymore. Dad! Dad! Mom, help!"

Climbing up the side of the pier, Nicole calmly told Missy to sit down, put her feet against the cleat, and hang on. "You're doing great, Missy."

Nicole grabbed the rope. "Call 911. Tell them we're at the Miller's cabin at Pelican Lake," she instructed Missy as she dragged Dave to the shore, which took only twenty seconds. On the beach, she administered CPR, thanking her lucky stars that she still remembered what she learned in nursing school years ago. A cough, a spitting of water, and a breath were music to her ears. She ripped off her soaking wet sweater, rung it out, and wrapped it tightly around the gash in Dave's head.

"I told them. They're coming," said Missy, running to them and looking at Dave in concern.

"Great. Now, find a couple of blankets in the cabin. Hurry," Nicole gave Missy further instructions, which she followed without a word. Nicole's demeanor, expressed in calm words and actions, helped eliminate any sense of panic in Missy.

What seemed like hours were only eight minutes, after which an ambulance arrived. Nicole let out a sigh of relief.

Dave, Nicole, and Missy waved goodbye as the ambulance drove away. With his arms tightly wrapped around his two favorite girls, he kissed Nicole on the cheek and Missy on her head.

She looked at him lovingly and said, "Mom saved your life, Dad." Dave could see admiration in her eyes for her mother, which Dave knew reflected in his eyes, too.

"Yes, I know. And she had excellent help, young lady. If not for both of you, and I mean *both* of you," Dave emphasized and continued, "I would be swimming with the fish."

Nicole smiled. Missy laughed. Dave said, "Missy, I'm sure glad you don't have to shave."

***

"Yeah, I remember that. She saved my life, didn't she?" Dave smiled at the memory.

"When she needs to, your cool-headed and competent wife takes charge. Right now, she's in charge of her situation," Brian tried to help him see some sense in the situation, hoping that he would approach whatever was going on with a cool head and not let his emotions cloud his judgments.

Looking sullen, Dave nodded in agreement.

To change the conversation, Brian read him the riot act, hoping to kick him out of his morose behavior. "Your job right now is to hit the damn ball long and far. If you don't, I'm out of here!"

Dave flinched. His emotions felt the kick as if it was in his butt. He felt like a child being scolded and an adult who needed to get their act together. He stuck out his lower lip, but his expression softened when he realized that Brian was only helping him, in the 'Brian way,' of course. Looking up, he nodded vigorously. "Thanks, Bri." He rubbed his butt and said, "It hurt, but I forgive you."

Brian liked Dave's words but wasn't sure his mind allowed him to think about golf rather than Nicole. He could only hope that his words and advice would push Dave to rethink whatever he was thinking and not get any deeper in misery than he already was.

"Okay," said Brian. " You're up. And, oh, you still need to tell me about your news. I didn't fly all the way here just to play golf with you." he added sarcastically, and Dave nodded at him with a smile in acknowledgment.

Chapter 14:

Ricochet

Dave meandered up to the tee. It struck Brian that he had as much energy as a sloth who just had his fill of leaves. After pushing his tee down, picking it up, pushing it down again, and placing his ball on the tee, then off the tee, then on the tee, he stepped back from the ball. Holding the grip of his driver and resting the shaft on his shoulder, Dave looked out at the fairway. He stepped forward, then back, then forward. Brian shook his head. He wished he had a cattle prod.

"Anytime you're ready, Dave," he called out, hoping that Dave would take a hint and be over with it already.

Dave hit his drive on the sixth hole and kept his head down well after the drive. He turned to Brian and said, "Did you see where it went?"

Deadpan, Brian said, "Sorry, I was fascinated by a couple of geese fighting. Did you get it on the fairway for a change?"

Dave shrugged. "I think so. It sounded good. It might be way, way out there. Don't know."

"Let me get my rangefinder to take a look." He scanned the fairway, paused, and said, "A-ha."

"What do you read?" Dave asked curiously, wanting to know the yardage to wherever Brian was pointing.

"Mostly science-fiction, and sometimes thrillers." He gave Dave a quick smirk. Dave was non-responsive. Brian shrugged, disappointed that Dave didn't laugh or even groan at his joke.

Brian drove his ball far and relatively straight. Coincidentally, both balls were only a few feet apart, about one hundred forty yards from the hole. "You're away, Dave. Go for it." No sooner did the words leave his mouth than Brian thought the *away* had more than one meaning. He wondered if Dave noticed or not. But given his off-mindedness in the past hour, he concluded that it was less likely that he would.

Brian watched his ball arching high, heading toward the pin. "Yeah, yeah," he said in a soft voice. "When you land my wonderful ball, bite!" It did bite on the green, but twenty feet away from the hole. "A-hem," said Brian proudly.

Dave didn't respond to Brian's braggadocios *A-hem*. Nonchalantly, he hit his ball without first taking a practice swing and without much attention to where he was aiming. A thud was heard when his ball faded and hit a tree trunk. As if he planned it, the shot ricocheted left and landed on the apron about thirty feet from the pin.

Wanting to make light of the errant but good shot, Brian gently smacked Dave's shoulder. "Now that's what I call ball control."

Dave raised his eyebrows and got into the golf car. Brian struggled with how to lift Dave's spirits. *Remind him that Nicole will be alright. Come down hard on him. Ignore him. Let him work it out.*

Knowing Dave got lucky with his shot, he decided to rib him. "You know it's lucky that you were good at tennis."

"Tennis?" Dave gave him a look as if almost disgusted at the thought, "I sucked at it."

Brian knew how Dave met Nicole. The whole story. He heard it several times. "I can't remember the entire story, but didn't you meet Nicole while playing tennis?

***

"You're going to love this, Dave. Maybe even give up golf," said Pete, Dave's classmate and buddy during their senior year at Northwestern.

"No way, Jose," Dave said with confidence. "Nothing can beat the thrill of golf, but I'll give it a try," he added. "I hope my experience is better than the one you had when I tried to teach you golf."

"Tennis is no different than golf, Dave. All you have to do is keep your eye on the ball and hit it back," Pete rolled his eyes.

"Pete, maybe my brain's not working, but I don't think a golf ball moves when you go to hit it. It sits there, mindless, not moving, just waiting for something to smack it," Dave emphasized with his hand gestures.

Dave wished he had read up on tennis and viewed some videos to learn how to play the game. Unlike the *be-prepared* Dave, Pete was a plunger. "The best way to learn, buddy, is to jump in."

Dave looked at the racquet Pete lent him, gripping it like a golf club. Pete noticed and was quick to instruct him, "One hand, Dave. It's not a golf club."

Swinging his racquet repeatedly, he realized the slight similarity to swinging a golf club or a baseball bat. Feeling confident he could control the racquet, he said, "Give me your best shot, Pete."

"Here we go, Dave." Pete's slow serve to Dave arched just over the net. Dave looked like he was dancing on burning coals as the ball approached. *Smash!* The ball rocketed toward Pete, just above his reach. Hitting the pole on the chain link fence, it ricocheted to the adjacent court.

"Fore!" screamed Dave when he saw his ball aiming for a player.

Pete was bent over laughing. "Kind of a funny shot, huh?" said Dave.

"No, not that. Fore?" Dave joined him in his laughter.

"This yours?" a feminine voice caught their attention. Dave turned to look at the young, attractive, athletic-looking lady as she held up a tennis ball.

"Yup. Sorry," Dave said sheepishly and muttered a "Thanks."

She smiled and handed it to him but didn't let go when his hand grabbed the ball. Their fingers touched. They looked at each other for two seconds, holding their stance, holding the ball. Dave cleared his throat.

She let go but kept her gaze. "Maybe you should stick to golf," she said and turned around to walk away.

"How do you know I play golf?" Dave's question stopped her midway, and she turned to look at him.

"Fore?" she raised her brows.

"Oh," Dave said, figuring she must have heard him yell as they played and laughed. "Yeah, I should. That's the first tennis ball I ever hit," Dave told her.

"I hope it's not your last, Dave," Nicole said with a grin.

"How do you know my name?" Dave asked.

"I'm psychic," Nicole said deadpanned.

His eyes lit up when he said, "I'm impressed."

Her lips curved into a sweet smile. "You should be."

"So tell me, psychic, what does this evening hold for us?"

With a coy smile, she said, "How are you with numbers?"

"Genius."

She rattled off her telephone number, turned, said her name was Nicole, and walked back to continue her game.

***

After the two-minute story that Dave recounted, Brian uttered *Ahh,* and said, "Yes, now I remember. Tennis. I especially like when you took off your golf shirt and saw your name on it."

"Isn't it interesting that your golf ball did the same thing your tennis ball did eons ago?" Brian looked at Dave.

145

"Coincidence. What's your point?" Dave asked, trying to get where this conversation was going.

"Important things, turning points if you will, stick in your head and come to life when the memory becomes useful. We have this knee-jerk reaction, more like a mind-jerk, to unlock a door and see what's behind it whenever there's a need," said Brian thoughtfully.

"Heavy stuff, Bri. I still don't get your point," Dave huffed.

"There are turning points in life. I had many, and I'm sure you did too. One of your big turning points was when you hit that tennis ball."

"You mean I wouldn't have met Nicole if I didn't," Dave frowned, almost finding it absurd.

Brian nodded.

Dave impassively looked at his ball but wasn't thinking about his putt. A dozen wonderful memories of his life with Nicole jetted by. He stood there, smiling.

"You okay, Davey boy?" asked Brian.

"Yeah, fine. I don't know why you wanted me to tell you how Nicole and I met. You knew how," Dave said. Brian could sense a slight annoyance in his tone but understood why his friend was being that way.

"You've been looking at your phone every five minutes. You just hit a shitty shot and didn't care. All I wanted to do was bring you back to reality. Let me ask you, why did you fall in love with Nicole?" Brian asked out of the blue. Dave wasn't expecting it, so he just concocted a vague answer.

"Whew. A ton of reasons," Dave shrugged, squinting his eyes as if trying to figure out which reasons stood out the most.

"Okay, give me a few pounds," Brian pushed.

Dave stuck his lips out, paused, uttered *Hmm*, and said, "Well__"

"By the way, Dave, I don't need them in alphabetical or chronological order."

Dave squinted and said, "A heart of gold, a brain that's always alert, eyes and a smile that shows her humanity…need more reasons?"

"Will she still have those qualities if, God forbid, she needs surgery?"

Dave stood still. His non-response was a response. Brian allowed Dave to chew on his words for a moment and then said, "Now putt the damn ball!"

Dave dropped his putter, walked to Brian, and hugged him. Brian hugged him back and said, "We're never going to finish this round if we keep hugging each other."

Smack! The ball jittered a bit on the apron's grass, went uphill onto the green, and turned a bit right as it went downhill toward the hole. *Plop!* "I love that sound when the ball drops in," said Dave. Hearing Dave's words was music to Brian's ears.

Back in their golf car, Dave recorded their score. "Did you have a par or bogey?" he asked.

"A birdie, I think. I don't know. I really don't give a shit. I just enjoy being with you and making fun of your golf game."

"Did you hear *fore?*"

"Nope."

They turned around in their seats to see if any players were coming up the fairway. *Bang!* A golf ball hit the top of their golf car. "Our bad. We shouldn't be sitting here. Off we go," said Dave.

"We're lucky it wasn't an F-16," said Brian.

They drove to the next hole, sipping their beverages and looking at the terrain. Brian appreciated the beauty of the golf course. It was lush with trees and flowering bushes planted on an immaculate grass carpet. He closed his eyes and took a prolonged breath to inhale the fresh air. He heard nature happening around him: goose wings slapping the water as they took to flight, birds chirping, a howling dog, or perhaps it was a coyote.

Brian's nirvana moment ended when Dave said, "I have a confession."

Chapter 15:

Confessions

Dave pulled off the car path, parking behind a huge tree trunk. Brian said, "Hmm. Confession. Let me guess. You're gay."

Dave slowly blinked and said, "I'm serious, and just in case that was a real question, no, I'm not gay."

"You're retiring. No, wait, you already did. You're taking a trip around the world like Charlotte and I did," Brian kept guessing, paying no heed to Dave's closed eyes and head shaking.

"Stop. I'm serious," Dave repeated. Brian looked at him, shaking his head a little before giving up. "Okay. Go for it."

"Remember about a thousand years ago when I arranged for that loan so you could start Sundance?" Dave began.

Brian wisely decided to stop trying to make a joke when he saw that his friend was dead serious. "Sure do. Got the loan at Ogilvie," Brian said, remembering what Dave was referring to.

"I wanted to arrange the loan with Hampton Investments. I thought they had better service," Dave finally revealed. It didn't sound like a great revelation to Brian after so much suspense and seriousness.

"Whew!" Brian let out an exaggerated sigh as he leaned back and extended his arms. "Of all the confessions I've heard in my lifetime, that is certainly one of them." He finished with a nod.

Dave shook his head, trying to keep the conversation serious. "You don't understand. I *had* to arrange it with Ogilvie. My boss told me to. I later found out she was friends with the lending officer at Ogilvie."

"Did I get screwed on the rate or the terms?" Brian looked at him, a bit concerned.

Dave waved his hand in dismissal, easing Brian's suspicion, and said, "No. No, you didn't. I just thought Ogilvie had better customer service,"

Brain shook his head. "What if Hampton had a lower rate or better terms? Would you still have recommended Ogilvie?"

Indignantly, Dave said, "Hell no! I wouldn't screw my friend."

"Job protection, right?" Brian continued to probe.

"Well, yeah. But you were my friend," Dave said.

"Were?" said Brian with a raised brow.

"Still are, you asshole."

Brian shook his head again. "Davey boy, you're something else. You did nothing wrong. You did everything right. You greased the wheels so I could get the loan. I got the loan. The terms were good. Nothing went wrong. So I am not accepting your confession."

"That's ridiculous. You can't deny someone confessing," Dave said in frustration, clearly not expecting the response he got from his best friend.

Brian lowered his head, his eyeballs riveted on Dave. "If you were in a church confessional booth telling that story, the priest would ask you to leave. When you come up with a real confession, I'll forgive you."

Dave did have a confession—a substantive one. Thoughts raced in his head. *Tell him that I lied about having news? Fabricate some news? Change the subject? Shouldn't Nicole be calling soon?* "Deal. When I have one, I'll let you know," Dave said after considering it.

"While we're confessing to each other, mostly you confessing, I have one for you," said Brian.

"Oh?" said Dave as he glanced at the time on his phone.

"She'll call," Brian interjected, knowing too well where his friend's mind was.

"You're confessing that she'll call?" Dave raised a brow, giving Brian a quizzical look.

Brian smiled. "Forget that. I knew about Hampton." That caught Dave's attention right away.

"How?" Dave asked, confused.

"Hampton contacted me just before I was going to sign with Ogilvie. I don't know how they knew about the loan," Brian told Dave and continued to look at him to see his reaction.

Dave turned toward Brian, engrossed in what Brian was saying. "What did Hampton say?" Dave was curious now. His thoughts and demeanor changed from meak confessor to bold inquisitor.

"What you said," Brian continued casually.

"What did I say?" Dave asked, frowning, trying to connect the dots.

"Is your memory going, young man?" Brian looked at him, perplexed. "You just told me why you recommended Ogilvie, not Hampton."

"Shit. How the hell did they know?" Gears spun in Dave's mind as he tried to figure it out.

Brian shrugged. "How the hell does anyone know what somebody else knows or what they know?"

Dave's mouth opened as if he was about to speak. His nose and brows scrunched. "Can you write that down so I can study it later?"

Brian laughed a genuine and hearty laugh. Dave didn't miss it. He smiled, huffed, and then joined in with his hearty laugh.

Dave said, "Of all the confessions I've heard in my lifetime__"

Brian cut him off with a "Shove it, bud."

Dave resumed his more relaxed posture behind the steering

wheel. "Can I tell you another confession that you might call real?"

Brian turned toward Dave, his index fingers pointing at his ears, his eyebrows raised.

"I lied about the reason for getting you here," Dave said sheepishly.

Brian sat back and looked up at the bottom of the golf car's roof. After a brief pause, he sighed and said in a softer tone, "I know exactly why you wanted me to come here."

"Who told you?" Dave asked.

"I bugged your house. I know everything you and Nicole said since you bought the place," Brian said sarcastically, maintaining his serious tone.

"Well, there you have it. No need to waste my words," Dave leaned back in his seat, understanding that Brian was back to his jesting.

Brian gently punched Dave in the arm. "I'm still all ears."

Dave paused. Hands clasped, looking down and twiddling his thumbs, he thought, *Should I blurt it out? He's acting like the Brian I knew. Friends are honest with each other. Why the hell did I bring it up?*

Brian looked at Dave, wondering what he was thinking while twiddling his thumbs. *The guy's a mess. Sure, Nicole. Never saw him like this. Is there something else going on?*

The beverage car pulled up next to them. "Need anything, gentlemen? I'm Beth, by the way."

They looked at her, and neither said a word. Dave had breasts on his mind. She noticed his glance. "How's it going out there?" she asked.

"Fine, I guess," said Dave.

Pointing at Dave, Brian said, "What he said."

"So, can I get you something?" asked Beth.

Dave and Brian didn't respond. Beth got confused, not knowing what to say to guys who acted strangely. She got out of the car and stirred up ice in the cooler to give them and herself a moment. Still not getting a response, Beth said, "See you later, then," and drove off, looking at her rearview mirror, wondering if they were just strange guys or just lost in thought.

Dave and Brian said the same thing at the same time: "You first." Giggling like teenagers, they raised their fisted hands with their pinkies sticking out. "She might be looking at us. We better not do that pinky thing," said Brian.

Brian broke the ice. "You're up, Dave. Confess your heart out."

Dave cleared his throat. "So, I lied about the reason for inviting you here."

"Yup. Heard that. And…?" Brian pushed.

"I was…ah…concerned. No, I was worried. Dammit, Bri! I thought you were going to try to kill yourself again," Dave blurted out and turned away to avoid Brian's gaze.

Brian looked at him with understanding and then said, "Good guess," making Dave turn to look at him. "But you're wrong. I wasn't going to try," Brian added. Dave looked askance at him and was about to say something when his phone vibrated and thrilled. He grabbed it off the dashboard compartment, and it fell to the ground. He jumped out of the car too fast and bumped his head on the roof.

"Dammit!" He bent down to retrieve his phone and found that it had landed in a slightly muddy area, face down. "For Christ's sake!" he shouted. Wiping off his phone, he saw that the text message was a solicitation from an air-conditioning company.

Brian saw him pulling his arm back as if he was about to throw his phone into the trees and said, "Easy, cowboy."

Dave stopped mid-way, inhaled deeply, and forcefully

emptied his lungs. "Another breath, Dave," Brian instructed.

Dave complied, calming down a little, and said, "Where were we? Oh, suicide."

Brian saw him looking at his phone and said, "I guess that wasn't Nicole calling."

He wiped the mud stain masking the time display on his phone. "No, she said she'd call 'bout two o'clock or as soon as she got the results. There should be a law against businesses calling you."

"Two more breaths might be in order," said Brian.

Following Brian's advice, Dave slightly slid down on his seat and visibly relaxed his body. "Close your eyes," save Brian. He did. "In through your nose, and slowly exhale through your mouth." He did. Five times. "Better?"

"Yeah. Breathing works," said Dave. "I gave the same instructions to Nicole when she was delivering Missy. In, out, in, out."

"Amazing how simple breathing can affect your mind and emotions," said Brian. "Let's just take a break. Breath in this warm, low-humidity Arizona air." With that, he got out of the cart and walked away to look at a bird with a broken wing. As he got closer, the wings flapped, and the bird bounced around but couldn't fly. He wanted to help the bird but couldn't think of anything to do that would be helpful. "I'm sorry, bird."

A ranger pulled up next to him. "Are you okay, sir?"

"Ah, yeah. Fine. Just taking a break," said Brian as he stepped out of the golf car.

The ranger looked at his notebook, touched the screen a few times, and asked, "Are you the Sherman twosome?"

"Yes. Is there a problem?" asked Brian.

"No. It's just that you're running late. You're two holes behind," said the ranger. The guys behind you asked me for lawn chairs."

Brian got the ranger's jovial sarcasm. Dave just kept cleaning his wristwatch and paid no attention to the banter. Brian glanced at the ranger's name badge. "Harry, you don't understand the situation. I'm teaching Mr. Sherman how to play golf. He's a very slow learner," Brian explained.

"I understand, sir, but the players behind you are being delayed, and__" the ranger began but was cut off by Brian.

"Harry, you don't understand. Mr. Sherman is deaf, and I'm not very good at sign language. Teaching takes time," Brian lied, a joke on his part, but he had to convince the ranger someway.

"Sorry, sir, but I need to suggest that you move along a little faster if at all possible," the ranger instructed. Clearly, Brian's effort to convince him didn't work.

"Got it. I'll do my best. I'll move my hands faster," Brian nodded.

Harry drove off, and Brian rejoined Dave in the golf car. "What's with the ranger," asked Dave.

"He told us to step it up, or the guys behind us are going to throw lawn chairs at us," said Brian.

Dave assumed Brian's mention of lawn chairs was one of his weird jokes, and chose to disregard it, and said, "So let's get moving," he said.

"Don't need to. I told him you had schizophrenia. You had to take a lot of breaks and remind yourself that you were playing golf."

Dave got out of the golf car and stood in front of it, looking and sounding angry. "Everything's a joke to you, isn't it?"

"No, not everything. Cool your jets, Dave," Brian slapped him on the shoulder.

Dave darted his finger on Brian's chest, keeping the beat with his words. You…just…don't…get it. Do you?"

Brian's blank stare bespoke his incredulity. He couldn't say a word. He got out of the car and stood in front of Dave, motionless. He didn't hear the birds chirping, the tree branches fluttering in the breeze, or Harry, the ranger who pulled up to them. From the looks of it, it was clear to Harry that Brian had lied to him about his friend being deaf.

"Really, guys?" said Harry. His words more than interrupted their confrontation. It gave them pause to quickly reflect on it.

"Bri. I am so so sorry," said Dave. He put his hands on Brian's shoulders. "I'm an idiot."

"No, you're not. I was an idiot," Brian shook his head.

"Fine. We're both idiots," Dave chuckled.

Looking at Dave, Harry said, "Glad you got your hearing back," and twisted his lips.

Brian aggressively pointed at Dave, and said, "Hit the road, Jack" and started singing, "'Hit the road, Jack, and don't you come back no more, no more, no more, no more.'"

Dave joined in the singing, "'Hit the road, Jack, and don't you come back no more.'"

They were delighted when they heard Harry bellow the next line, sounding very much like Ray Charles, "'What you say?'"

Chapter 16:

The Turn

They stopped at the next hole, got out of the golf car, and stood by their golf bags for nearly a minute, not saying a word. Both looked at the tranquil and lush terrain of the golf course, the geese pecking at the grass, ducks casually swimming in a pond, and a flock of birds flying by in formation. Brian broke the silence and said, "Yup."

"Yup," countered Dave.

While looking beyond the golf course at South Mountain in the distance, Brian asked, "What hole are we on now?"

"I'm not even sure I know what golf course I'm on," said Dave. "I think I've had it with golf today."

Brian didn't know what to say besides what he already said and decided to say "Redundancy."

"What about it? What's redundant?" asked Dave, clearly confused by the usage of the word in the situation.

Brian snorted. "I've been subpoenaed."

"Is this a joke?" Dave looked at him, resigned.

Brian looked squarely into Dave's eyes. "I'm not kidding. The Federal Department of Redundancy Department has subpoenaed me." He waited for a punch in the arm, a groan, or both.

Dave paused for a moment, digesting what Brian said. "You had me, Bri. Groan, groan. Is the second groan redundant?"

Brian smiled, glad that he broke Dave's train of thought. Glad they had it out. "I'm with you, bud. Let's call it a day."

Dave nodded, and both got into the golf car. Dave accelerated, and Brian asked him to stop. "Whadup, Bri?"

"The tunnel up ahead. Do we have to go through that tunnel?"

asked Brian.

It struck Dave that Brian had a problem, perhaps with claustrophobia. He never knew that about Brian. "Well, I don't know this course, but I'm sure we could drive around and find a way to avoid the tunnel. Claustrophobia, Bri?"

"No, not that. I suffer from CPTS – car path tunnel syndrome."

Dave uttered a combination of *uhh* and laughter as he shook his head. "You had me, you sick puppy." Brian crossed his arms, leaned back, and gave Dave a smug smile.

They drove on the car path that eventually would lead them to the locker rooms. At the halfway point, they spied what appeared to be an adobe-style house in the middle of the golf course. "Now that's what I call prime property," said Brian, clearly impressed by what he was looking at. "Smack in the middle of the golf course."

"Nope. It's the snack shack," said Dave. "Quite something, isn't it?"

"Yup. I could use some food. How about you?" Brian said and looked at Dave.

Dave looked at the time on his phone. It was still another hour until Nicole was supposed to have her test results. "Good idea. Let's see what they have."

They both got out of the car and walked toward the snack shack. The sign over the entry door read *Turn*. Both thought the name was prophetic but for different reasons.

Inside the air-conditioned *Turn,* they were surprised to see tables and chairs and a buffet-like set-up for wrapped sandwiches, mixed salads in containers, and beverages neatly displayed in a massive ice chest. "We also have burgers and hot dogs if you want something hot," said the attendant behind the buffet bar.

"I can see what Lenny meant," said Dave. "Quite a surprise."

"Life's a surprise, Dave. Lots of turns in life," Brian added.

They went through the menu, and Brian decided to order a cheeseburger; Dave went for a roast beef sandwich. After placing their orders, they sat next to a window looking out at the 10th tee, munching their food, making remarks about the golfers' stances and swings, and, a couple of times, about their golf clothes. In the meantime, their orders arrived, and they both dug in.

"We seem to be avoiding serious discussion," said Bri.

Dave chewed on his sandwich and the day's happenings. *Quite a turn of events,* he thought. He swallowed and said, "I'm a bit drained, my friend."

"I understand," Brian said, nodding, and popped a fry in his mouth, savoring the saltiness. Leaning forward, Dave continued, "I invited you here because everything I tried to tell you on the phone for the last few months seemed to have fallen on deaf ears."

"My hearing was fine. My *want* to hear, well, you know," Brian emphasized.

"I'm not finished," said Dave. He grabbed his beer, wobbled it on the table, looked down, and said, "I feel like I failed you as a friend."

"Bullshit! You're a great friend." Brian took a deep breath, curled his lips, and slowly exhaled. "You taught me something today. You told me to find the bright side and look at it. That's my new mantra."

Dave smiled as he felt the warmth of Brian's words, yet he felt unsettled with his accomplishment. "We've known each other for…forever. We've been friends for all of that time. I was desperate to convince you that you shouldn't…well, you know. But that Frank guy, that pastor, convinced you."

"Look at me. Look at me, dammit!" Brian didn't realize his voice was louder than it should have been. A couple of golfers ten feet away looked at him. He nodded and smiled at them. "I just wanted him to check my mascara." The golfers smiled.

Dave looked at him, eye to eye. Lowering his voice, he said, "I heard every word you said to me since yesterday. All of it, and I mean all of it, was convincing me that I made a mistake in trying to end my life."

"And Frank?" he added.

"Dave. Frank just added some icing. You made the cake. A great cake," Brian said, pointing at Dave. Dave's eyes started to well up with tears. His lips showed a slight quiver. "Now cut the shit. I'm here. Not going anywhere. And it's my turn," Brian said with conviction.

"Your turn for what?" Dave asked, looking a bit irritated. He couldn't understand why Dave thought he owed him something.

"To help you," Brian said softly. His tone and determination melted Dave's heart and made him believe he wasn't alone.

Dave nodded. "Yeah. I heard you. Everything you said convinced me that everything will turn out okay, regardless of what turns out."

"You're stealing my lines, asshole," Brian scrunched his brows.

Dave turned up his golf shirt and wiped his eyes. He grabbed his beer and held it up. "To you, my friend."

Brian picked up his beer. The bottles clinked. Two heads nodded. Dave's phone rang at the same time a guy called out, "Dad. Dad!"

Dave saw it was Nicole calling. He answered with "Hey" as he walked outside.

The guy who called out 'Dad' was Tom, Brian's son.

Recognizing the voice but not seeing the face, Brian called out, "Tom?"

Tom appeared from behind a pillar, and Brian's face lit up

when he saw him. He got up from his chair immediately and hugged him.

"What a surprise. What are you doing here?!" Brian asked Tom. Tom told him why he was in Scottsdale and how things got delayed, allowing him to visit. "How did you know I was here?"

"Aunt Nicole told me. The pro shop told me your golf car was parked here. The ranger gave me a lift. Whallah!" Where's Uncle Dave?"

Brian pointed out the window to where Dave was speaking on the phone. He saw him smiling and bowing with *yes* gestures. He gestured toward the window and said, "The guy out there jumping up and down is your uncle." He's my fourth leg."

Tom wasn't familiar with the expression but thought it might be a golf term or an inside joke. "I'll bite. Fourth leg?"

Brian snorted and told Tom it was an expression geezers used and hoped Tom never needed one. Tom remained in the dark and let it go.

In the *Turn,* Dave told Brian that the nodule was not cancer and that there was nothing to worry about. "I know," said Brian.

Laughing, Dave said, "Did you also bug my phone?" He turned to Tom. With a shocked look on his face, he said, "Tom. You're here. That's a stupid thing to say. What a great surprise."

"I spoke with Aunt Nicole this morning. That's how I knew you were here. She didn't say anything about cancer."

"Of course not. Why lay that on you?" said Dave.

"Got something to show you, Dad." Tom showed him a photo on his phone of his son, Gerry, holding a trophy. "First place in the Libertyville Freedom Tournament."

"I'm not surprised. I taught him how to play golf."

Dave cleared his throat loudly. "You're forgetting all the lessons I gave him."

Tom said, "Dad. Uncle Dave. If not for you two guys, Gerry would have had only one teacher, me, and I'm not what you would call a great golfer."

The guys laughed, drank their beers, and chatted about recent events. Tom pointed to the walls and said, "Great paintings." Dave and Brian laughed.

"Why are you laughing?" asked Tom.

Brian said, "Yeah, we like those nude paintings too."

Tom knew there was a joke somewhere within his dad's statement but chose to comment rather than ask. "I really like the one with the bobcats. The coyote one is also good."

Dave said, "They're all nude," and laughed. Brian joined in the laughter. Tom sat quietly.

"I have some news, guys," said Brian. "I'm selling the house in Seattle and moving to Chicago."

Dave gagged on his beer and coughed several times.

"I didn't know that," Tom said, frowning, not knowing what his dad had planned. "When did you decide to do that?" he asked.

"It's been on my bucket list," responded Brian with a shrug.

"Bucket list?" asked Dave. "I didn't even know you had a bucket."

Laughing, Brian said, "Yup. Got the bucket today. Kind of a symbolic bucket. They're cheaper than a real bucket but work just as well. I put a note in it to move. I want to be close to Gerry to improve his golf game."

"Here's a coincidence," said Dave.

Tom turned to Dave. "You're moving too, Uncle Dave?"

"No, no, no. The coincidence is that we're talking about a turn of events in a place called *Turn*," Dave clarified.

"Heavy," said Brian, looking smug.

Dave and Brian paused in conversation, looking down and

holding their beers. Had Tom been sitting between them, he would have felt their warmth. He gave them a moment for whatever they were reflecting on and said, "Turn. Great word. Lots of definitions. Turn the lights off. Something will turn up. Turn your life around. Turn__"

"Yeah, lots of definitions," said Dave.

"So, how have you guys played today?" asked Tom.

Brian cleared his throat and took another swallow of beer. "Your uncle was about to confess something to me just before you got here." He exaggerated his smile and looked at Dave.

"Hmm," said Dave. He leaned forward closer to Brian and Tom. He looked around the room and whispered, "I don't floss every day."

Tom smiled out of courtesy, not knowing if it was an inside joke or detour. "No, I do have a confession. Well, it's more like news, I guess. We're taking a page out of your book, Bri. Nicole and I are planning to take a trip around the world. It's on our bucket list."

"I didn't know you had a bucket," said Brian. Tom closed his eyes and shook his head.

"We're even on not knowing about each other's bucket." He took a swig of his beer. "By the way, my bucket's bigger than your bucket!"

Tom thought, *Am I going to act this way in thirty years?* He decided to pipe in on the nonsensical jabs and counter-punches. "I can see why you guys are friends." He raised his beer and nodded at them.

"So, really, how did you guys play today?"

Dave and Brian gave Tom a topline of the great shots they made, how Brian helped some young weed-smoking drunks, and how they shared memories of their lives for the past fifty-seven years. "Funny," said Brian. "I look back at all those years, all those events, and sometimes think it was all meant to be."

"You mean destined to be?" asked Tom.

"Kinda," Brian nodded.

"I don't agree, Bri," said Dave. We're not characters in a book where some author decided how we should act or feel."

Tom wasn't aware that thoughts were rocketing in their heads about the day's events. The ups and downs. The reliving. The anguish. The revelations. "Talk about heavy statements, wow," said Tom.

"Glenfarclas at my place?" asked Dave, looking at Brian while nodding, signaling his want for Brian to agree.

Is that Gaelic?" asked Tom.

Dave and Brian laughed loudly. Tom's confused look made them laugh even louder.

They rose, and with Tom in the middle they held their arms around each other's shoulders as they walked from *Turn* to a life to live for.

Glossary

Address (the ball) – Taking a stance by the ball, gripping the club, and setting your posture before hitting the ball.

Apron – The grass surface on the perimeter of the green that separates it from the surrounding fairway or rough.

Away – Applicable only after players hit their ball from the tee; the player farthest from the hole is the first to play.

Backswing – The motion of taking the club away from the ball by swinging it backward in preparation for swinging the club forward to hit the ball.

Backspin – The spin of the ball produced by contact with the clubface. A ball with a backspin will typically fly higher and, therefore, stop or spin backward on impact with the turf.

Bagboy – A soon-to-be outdated term for a golf bag attendant who helps golfers load and unload their clubs on a golf car and cleans golf club heads and other duties, depending on the golf course policies.

Balance – The proper distribution of the golfer's body weight while *addressing* the ball and throughout the swing.

Beach – Term used for a sand bunker.

Birdie – A score of one under *par* on a hole. Also called a **Bird**.

Bite – The backspin on a ball that makes it stop dead, or almost so, when it lands.

Bladed Shot – A shot when the golf club strikes the top half of the golf ball. Also called a **Thin Shot**.

Bogey – A score of one over par on a hole.

Bump and Run – A *pitch* shot around the *green* in which the player hits the ball into a slope to deaden its speed before settling on the green.

Bunker – A hollow usually filled with sand. Also called a **Sand Trap**.

Bunker Shot – Hitting the ball out of a bunker (sand trap) onto the *green* or *fairway*.

Caddie – A person who carries clubs for the golfer and often provides advice on how and where to hit a ball.

Callaway – A brand name of golf clubs, golf balls, and golf paraphernalia.

Carry – The distance from the spot from which a ball is hit to where it first hits the ground. If the ball continues to move forward after it hits the ground, the point at which it stops is the distance the ball traveled.

Chicken Wing – A bent lead elbow pointing away from the body when the club is about to hit the ball.

Chip (Shot) (Chipping) – A shot played from close to the *green* that results in the ball popping briefly into the air, then hitting the ground and rolling toward the hole.

Chunk – A poor shot caused by hitting the turf well behind the ball. Also called a **Fat Shot**.

Cup – The hole on the green that is the ultimate target for the ball.

Dance Floor – Slang for when your golf ball is on the green.

Divot – The small chunk of turf that is displaced when the club strikes the ball on a descending path.

Dogleg - A hole where the *fairway* is crooked or bends like a dog's hind leg.

Dog Track – A derogatory term for a golf course that is not well maintained.

Double Bogey – A score of two over par.

Double Eagle – A score of three under par on a hole. Also called an **Albatross**.

Downhill Putt / Uphill Putt -- The slope of the green and the condition of the grass (short grass, well groomed, moisture, etc.) affects the ball's speed and trajectory when hit. For a downhill putt, the ball should be hit softer than for an uphill putt because gravity accelerates the ball's velocity.

Downswing – The swing forward from the top of the backswing.

Draw – A shot that flies slightly from right to left, as opposed to a **Fade**.

Drive – The first shot taken from the tee box at each hole.

Driver - A club designed to produce the most distance when a ball is struck. Also see **Woods**.

Driving Range – See **Practice Range**.

Drop - A golfer typically takes a drop after hitting his ball in an area where another shot cannot be played – e.g. if the ball is in a creek. The ball must be dropped straight down from knee height onto a selected area from where the ball can be hit.

Eagle – A score of two under par.

Fade – A shot that flies slightly from the left to the right. Also, see **Draw**.

Fairway – The closely mowed area between the *tee box* and the *putting green*.

Fat Shot – Striking the ground behind the ball, resulting in poor contact with the ball and less yardage than if the ball was struck and then the ground.

Flag – See **Pin**. Used to denote where a hole is located on a *green*. It is placed in the hole and extends up several feet above the ground, ensuring that players on the course can locate the position of the hole from several hundred yards out to best aim their approaches. Also known as a **Pin**

Flop Shot – A high lofted greenside golf shot with almost no roll.

Follow-through – That part of the swing that occurs after the ball has been struck.

Fore – Shouted to warn anyone standing or moving in the flight of a golf ball.

Forward Swing – The downward motion of the hands, arms, and club from the top of the *backswing*.

Foursome – A group of four players.

Fried Egg – Slang for a ball half-buried in the sand in a bunker.

Fringe – See **Apron**.

Gimmie – A putt that other players in the group that are playing together agree that it counts as made without it being played.

Green – See **Putting Green**.

Grip it and Rip it – A common expression for hitting a ball, usually with a driver, as forcefully as possible.

Gross Score – The total score (number of strokes) for a round of golf. Also, see **Net Score.**

Handicap – A number that represents a golfer's ability based on their previous rounds' scores. If a player shoots a score of 80 for an 18-hole round of golf and has a 10 handicap, the *net* score for the round is 70.

Hole-in-one – Hitting the ball once from the tee box into the cup (the hole) on the green.

Hybrid(s) Golf Clubs – A cross between an **Iron** and a **Fairway Wood**.

Intended Line of Flight – The direction in which a player plans for the ball to begin its flight after impact.

Inbounds - A ball is inbounds when any part of the ball lies on or touches the ground or anything else (such as any natural or artificial object) inside the boundary edge of the golf course.

Iron(s) - A golf club that usually has smaller clubheads than *woods*. The head is typically made of solid iron or steel.

Lie – The position of the ball where it landed and the ground condition at that point.

Links – Technically, a type of golf course usually located on coastal dunes. 'Links' is also a casual reference (jargon) for all golf courses.

LIV – A professional men's golf tour. The name 'LIV' refers to the Roman numeral 54 - the number of holes played at LIV events.

Loft (of a golf club) – The degree of angle on the clubface, with the least loft on a *putter* and the most, usually, on a *sand wedge*.

Loft (of a ball's flight) – The maximum height (apex) of a ball's trajectory.

Match Play – A form of play where a player (or players) plays directly against an opponent (or opponents) in a head-to-head match. You win a hole by completing it in the fewest number of strokes, and you win a match when you are winning by more holes than remain to be played.

Mulligan – The custom of hitting a second ball on a hole without penalty.

Net (score) – The *gross score* for a round of golf minus the number of handicap strokes received according to one's course handicap.

Par – The score a player is expected to make on a hole – three, four, or five, and rarely, six.

PGA -- The PGA Tour is the organizer of professional golf tours in the United States and North America.

Pin – Used to denote where a hole is located on a *green*. The flag stick is placed in the hole and extends up several feet so players can see where the hole is located from a long distance. Also called **Flag**.

Pin High – Hitting the golf ball on or near the green level to the distance of the pin. Your ball can be left or right of the pin but not in the hole.

Ping – A brand name of golf clubs and golf paraphernalia.

Pitching (Pitch, Pitch Shot) – A short shot with (usually) a high trajectory.

Pitching Wedge - A golf club used to hit a shot with a high and short trajectory.

Play(ing) Through – Players in one group move ahead of the players in another group if the other group is playing very slowly. Permission is typically granted.

Pop-up – A hit ball that pops up high into the air and typically travels a shorter distance forward than expected, because contact happened at the very top of the clubface. Also called a **Skyball.**

Practice Range -- An area equipped with distance markers, sometimes golf clubs, balls, and tees for practicing golf shots. Also called a **Driving Range**.

Punch -- A shot that is played with the intent of lowering the golf ball's trajectory in flight.

Push – The term indicating that both players in (typically) *Match Play* had the same score on a given hole – i.e., neither player won the hole.

Putt – A golf stroke used with a putter when the golf ball is on or just off the green

Putter – The club used to make low-speed strokes to roll the ball into the hole from a short distance away.

Putting Green - A smooth grassy area at the end of a golf **Fairway** containing the hole.

Range Finder – A device used to measure the distance to a remote object, such as from where you are standing to where the pin is.

Retriever (Golf Ball Retriever) – A long pole, typically collapsible, with a scoop or claw on the end to retrieve golf balls (from water, down embankments, anywhere they are hard to reach).

Rough – The area of grass that typically borders a fairway but which is deliberately kept longer than that of the fairway grass.

Sand Trap – See **Bunker**.

Sand Wedge - A heavy, lofted iron with a flange on the bottom, used for hitting the ball out of the sand.

Scratch Golfer – Generally defined as a person who has a 0.0 or better handicap or often shoots around even par.

Skyball – See **Pop-up**.

Slice – A ball that curves from left to right more than a *fade*.

Sweet Spot – The center of the face of a golf club where the golf ball should be hit for optimal results.

TaylorMade – A brand name of golf clubs and golf paraphernalia.

Tee - A stand used to elevate a stationary ball prior to striking it with a club.

Tee Box - The starting point on every hole of the golf course – the place from which golfers play the first stroke of each hole.

Tee off – To hit a ball off the tee box with or without a tee. The term is often used to cite the time of the start of a round of golf.

Tee Time – The reserved time that a golfer is scheduled to hit the first ball in a round of golf.

Teeing Up – Placing a ball on a tee.

Thread the Needle – A perfect shot that was placed between obstacles, such as tree trunks.

Threesome – A group of three players.

Trajectory - The height and angle at which the ball travels when struck.

Trap – See **Bunker**.

Turn – An expression used to denote the 'halfway point' on an 18-hole golf course, where the first nine holes have been played, and holes 10-18 remain to be played.

Twosome – A group of two players.

Up and Down – The act of taking just two strokes to get your golf ball into the hole when your ball is resting around the green or in a greenside bunker.

Uphill Putt / Downhill Putt -- The slope of the green and the condition of the grass (short grass, well groomed, moisture, etc.) affects the ball's speed when hit. For an uphill putt, the ball should be hit harder than for a downhill putt because gravity will slow the ball's velocity.

Wedge – Any of several different irons designed for specific situations where a high loft shot with a relatively short distance is required.

Wood(s) - A golf club used to hit the ball longer distances than irons. In addition to a *driver,* the most common woods are 3, 5, and 7.

Yard (Yardage) – Each hole is measured in straight lines from a permanent marker on the tee box to the center of the green. In Dogleg holes, a measurement is taken from the tee box to the pivot point in the fairway, and a second measurement from that point to the center of the green.